PRETTY

LIES

PERISH

FRANK CERVI

"If honesty were suddenly introduced into American life, the whole system would collapse."

- George Carlin

"The world says: "You have needs -- satisfy them. You have as much right as the rich and the mighty. Don't hesitate to satisfy your needs; indeed, expand your needs and demand more." This is the worldly doctrine of today. And they believe that this is freedom. The result for the rich is isolation and suicide, for the poor, envy and murder."

-Fyodor Dostoyevsky,
The Brothers Karamazov

CONTENTS

THE INTERSTATE

Gainesville, Florida, 1985

A tangled knot of concrete and design stands in the near distance: a turnpike that seems to unwind towards any freedom. The traffic light is red in front of me as I look up and wonder if sunsets are like snowflakes, that if any one of them throughout history has ever been exactly like this one; the same clouds, in the exact same spots, being radiated by the crimson fire of all the electric oranges, yellows and reds that highlight their outer edges.

I hear the impatient honking - liberal use of the horn- of some fucking prick behind me as I realize I've been stuck in this thought longer than I should. The light is now green along with its side kick; the white man that also confirms my Ford F-250 should be in motion as pedestrians walk inside those parallel lines like good little citizens. The guy behind me is still an asshole though- he just flipped me the bird. Fuck 'em, what a cocksucker. His anger is most likely stemming from the loss of his job, his wife or that he's late for happy hour; the only night off from the tykes at home while some Madonna, wannabe teen, takes care of them for a dismal token. It's anyone's guess really. Everyone has a story that they alone know the real truth too; always hidden beneath the frown, smile, random fits of anger, or aloofness. The rest of us just make up the narrative for them regardless.

People are so impatient today. Where are you going that is so pressing that you have no patience for my retarded start at some intersection in Gainesville of all places? Certainly to go get a load on, score some powder. It is 7:10 p.m. and what else can one do down here? It's a town just as any other in this great state, generic; full of the same thoughts, same homes, same jobs, and same beliefs. Stray animal's litter its bushes, alleyways and streets; walking with carnal purpose on some kind of auto pilot. Nobody cares for them; they don't even care for themselves. So why should anyone? The guy in front of me has remnants of road varmint mashed under his right rear tire.

As I merge onto I-75 North, I scroll between the dials, scrambling over radio talk shows mentally masturbating about how President Regan's economic policies have turned this country around in the last five years, and then skipped over a station out of Valdosta mentioning that some local girls gone missing. I finally settle on some tower out of Jacksonville that's playing Def Leppard's new song "Animal." The singer's voice comes through my speakers in and out of static then into clarity; guitars harmonically picking, the bass of those drums a primitive beat.

As a kid growing up I used to take road trips just like this one all the time with my old man in his Oldsmobile. He was a drunk, and took a shine towards gambling whatever savings he had. My mother left us when I was just old enough to understand why she got tired of my old man's shit. I don't know where she is or how she is surviving, perhaps just like everyone else or worse.

We didn't say much to each other the whole way on those trips to Atlanta, Jacksonville, Tampa; he liked to drive in quiet, and I didn't mind being stuck in my own head. I remember staring out the window, the warm Gulf air with its heavy grip around my hair and the sun blanketing road before us, just thinking about its nature.

I remember one time having to stop on the shoulder of the interstate because my old man had to throw a piss from all the cans of Lone Star or Old Milwaukee that littered beneath our feet, his version of Father of the Year. When we had to stop, I would stay in the car with the windows up, feeling the vibrations of the tankers that flew by, and the white noise of engines and the heavy bass of their velocities, feeling as if I were inside of some giant beast and hearing its heartbeat.

Man built roads and highways first and foremost to connect infrastructure, to produce commerce and effective travel. We made the world smaller, we wanted to see people and more often. Even during the times when there were no roads or paths, man would carve his own, and others would travel on his imprint like how ants follow one another's scent; an instinct unbreakable.

The interstate is a living breathing animal; it's a machine, a system to which has its own laws, codes and life force to insure its maintenance and survival.

Signs sending signals of where to go, gas stations to keep the flow of endless traffic to which trespasses through its veins to ensure it never clogs.

Blue lights circle and flash in my rear-view, ricocheting around the inside on all surfaces. I am not speeding nor have I had a drink tonight but I still feel the cold surge of electricity up my neck, a twinge of anxiety. A State Trooper- the highways white blood cell.

I slow my truck to a dead stop on the shoulder just outside of the Florida-Georgia border. I can hear that heartbeat of the beast as the cars and trucks stream by, the strobes behind me. My window gets stuck half way down when I try to roll it as I hear the clicking of the trooper's boots as they hit the pavement in lock step --- a man in his mid-forties, for sure. It's probably the start of a shift for him. Trying to feel out the mood of the road and who is out here tonight.

"What seems to be that matter office..."He cuts me off almost immediately. He either has a chip on his shoulder or is trying to assert his dominance immediately. Who knows, maybe his wife just left him. I can see the tan line of a ring; divorced recent perhaps. Or maybe he takes it off to score strange at one of these flee ridden motels out here on the fringes; regardless, what a prick.

He uses one finger through his leather glove to stress the point, "First thing, never roll down your window unless I ask you son. You wait until I tell you to do something for my safety and yours. License and registration please," he said with an air of machismo.

I hand over my plastic to him confidently. Nothing to hide I thought, no booze on my breath, yet. "Yes officer, I understand sir. It won't happen again. What seems to be the matter?" I reiterate.

"Couldn't make out your plate, it's got rust all on it. Hard to tell who's who and what's what out here if that's the case boy." He said with an annoyed tone. I could barely make out his name and badge since dusk was now settling into complete night.

"My apologies, Officer... Boswell, I hadn't got it fixed just yet, been meaning too though."

He fires off again this time, less stern, "Where are you heading tonight son? I only ask because I can tell you are crossing state lines and I can't guarantee them troopers over in Georgia will treat you different."

As I register this first sign of humility from him I begin to look over him more closely; resembling some failed or retired pilot from the movie Top Gun. His face like an old catcher's mitt beneath the Aviators, salt and pepper patches of fur make up his 5 O'clock. "Going to Valdosta Officer," I said calmly. "Going there to find something I guess."

"Aren't we all now, trying to find that *something*." He said whist flipping his paper pad shut.

"Well son, you better find a new license plate soon because if I catch you out here in these parts again, with this sorry looking piece, you can be sure I won't be as easy as I am being on this night."

"You got it Officer, thanks" I said in liberation.

I am in no hurry and have no time to waste, he did though: Inefficiency in the system. A sense of relief washes over me, and I wait for him to pull out first. The strobes are off and its business as usual.

***

Valdosta, Georgia 8:32 P.M.

The border sign up ahead reads WELCOME: WE'RE GLAD GEROGIA'S ON YOUR MIND. The night has made its way into the sky; those electric colors have long disappeared from its canvas. A full moon reflects its light through partial clouds like a spot light over the roads cracks and imperfections. A sign carries the message of gas and cheap vacancy off the next exit to which I submit to as a final resting stop for this night.

The rest-area outside of Valdosta looks like a small village or outpost teeming with all the elements of a highway at this hour of night, a collector of all the vagrants, truckers, dope runners, prostitutes and the occasional family looking for a place for a quick bite before they make their way to the Sunshine state for Spring Break- A mix of Canadians and northern state folk for this time of year.

I could care less about the activities; I just need some bottles of J&B, some food and a motel room for the night. There is motel up ahead over a slight hill in the road, THE BIG 8 which is next to a service station. The parking lot is sparsely filled: a few Fords, a black 85' Buick Grand National, some Harleys and a dark red 85' El Camino. It ain't the weekend just yet.

I think about motels for a minute as a flick of my lighter breathes life into one of my Belmont's. A girl no older than 17-18 in a tight black skirt, and garnished red stilettos, steps out of a truck's cab only to strut to the next rig beside it and disappear. I honestly don't remember the first time I stayed in a motel. And of course, that means I have no clue where I was the first time that happened. To me motels are interesting places.

Much of the time, the license plates of the cars in the parking lot are not from the state where the motel is sited. Most of us who park in the motel parking lot are strangers to the place, and strangers to the others who are going to be our motel-mates for the night. When you check in, you might spy two or three others who are going to share your building for the night. But for the most part, you do not even see the others.

A motel stay is temporary. Temporarily, I know that the place has been prepared for me. And if I stay more than one night, I know that I will leave in the morning and mysteriously someone appears in my room, makes the bed, etc. and vanishes. In fact, I realize every person who works for the motel is there to serve me. I still don't quite know how to deal with this. I grew up learning I was supposed to take care of myself, be independent, and don't expect others to do things for me. A motel turns that assumption upside down. Motels are for transients, that is, motels are where those passing through choose to stay. Our residence is temporary. We do *not* "settle in."

Taking two final drags from my cig, I stamp it out on the broken concrete that lay before my boots. That girl in the red stilettos emerges from the rig, dishevelled, adjusting her attire, all the while her make-up starting to languish like the blue paint on the bricks of the motel. Her gaze interrupts my thoughts as almost to signal that I can have a turn if I should choose, but I give her my wink and make my way to the motel desk; neon lamps and the sign of vacancy flicker, casting red and blue light over the entrance way. My boots clicking the gravel mixed with pavement beneath me.

That girl is a symptom of this country's struggle to survive, a pre-programmed intuition that most of her type have in this country; an evolved form of deception and con from our primate relatives. The strut she gave coming out of that big rig, the arched back and those heels that made her ass stick out like a shining beacon telling all tall ships to make port: the Lordosis Complex. With make-up, she can make it look like she's always about to drop an egg and even exaggerate an effect that would normally be subtle.

The harder she's trying to get things from men, the more make-up she uses. She is a predatory female, the kind that tries to survive these parts, and you can't blame her. It's scratch and claw out here. They prey on man's desire and archaic panache for females in heat, or in this case, the *illusion* that they are in heat. Going into season every month makes the human females unusual among animals, but they are only really fertile a few days each cycle. The other ninety percent of the time, men are getting played.

With most animals, it's blatantly obvious when the female is ready to ovulate, and she never lies. With humans, it's nearly the opposite. Men play a con as well in the form of the illusion of wealth, our fancy cars, comfy jobs and suits. Nothing is so secure in this world, not beauty, and most of all wealth and security. It can all be taken away from us in an instant. Nature knows no bounds or rules set by man.

As I walk into the motel lobby, towards the front desk, I can hear "Sentimental Street" by Night Ranger faintly from the radio in the corner on a table next to some travel magazines. I ring the bell and it takes almost a minute before some old woman emerges out of the darkened backroom, like some sea urchin from a cavern beneath watery depths. She gives a half-hearted smile which makes her wrinkled face look like some sort of a past due pumpkin as she opens up her manifest.

"Just you tonight sugar?" she says in a voice that doesn't match the decay in her beauty. An odd moment of clarity of how we don't become old, only our bodies do.

"That's right ma'am, I'm flying solo."

"Interesting my dear, a handsome guy like you and no gal being by your side," She expressed this with all the charm an old woman like her could muster; a compliment nonetheless.

"Not tonight ma'am. But I can see this ain't a lonely place for a travelling man," I motioned with a hint of sly cheekiness, nodding and angling my head towards the big rigs outside.

"You have that right my dear. Well its $30 for the room tonight, $150 if you are staying the week. No extra if you decide to have a friend in their hun, that's between you and them. Just don't make a party of it m'kay?"

I place a twenty down along with five dollar bills on the counter while reaching for another 5 in my back pocket as the song on the radio switches to Springsteen's "Badlands." One of the bills is crumpled and weathered, and I wonder how far it has travelled around this country, which places it has been, and how many G-strings it has nestled in.

"Just the night, that's great handsome just fill out the ledger here with your name and address," she says as she moves some papers aside to make room for my use.

As I finish making my mark, I look up at the cheesy clock on the wall above and realize I haven't eaten in a while; my stomach feeling empty needing to be filled with meat and booze. The old woman then confirms the registration in much routine to her voice. "#6 is the room dear; pass that soda machine there at the end. Enjoy your stay with us here at The Big 8, Mr. Cobb."

I gave her a flick of my ball cap that read "Florida Gator's," while I casually slipped the motel key into my right jean pocket leaving the lanyard out a bit for easy access, and headed out the door.

I took a step outside to observe my surroundings and lit another Belmont before planning to make my way across the road to a pub; it was nicely placed beside a store that read "Liquor" on the front in a bright flamboyant marquee- American convenience at its finest.

The air is calm tonight but hangs over everything like a heavy blanket. I can feel the humidity tighten my chest, sweat starts to form above my brow, and it's hard to breath. Smoking doesn't help the situation. I look once again around the pumps towards the big rigs at the service station parked in rows that resemble an orderly assembly.

A different girl hops out of an older model Mack rig and strolls off towards the bathrooms, probably to get rid of that trucker's effluence that's either in or on her. The driver steps off his rig, lights up a smoke and re-adjusts his crotch; another satisfied customer.

I don't judge him or her. He being on the road and all; must get to you after awhile seeing the same signs, lines and occurrences of the highway life. The girl, most likely a stray or a runaway; the kind you find in the bushes, alleyways and on street corners pulling tricks even just for a place to stay the night. Most of them don't even know why they are out here short of a of rebel reflex. Even if they choose to go back to the roost it's usually too late for them. That life consumes your worth; there is nothing glorious about any of it. You are lucky if you make it to your 25th birthday out here between all the pimps, rapists, gang-bangers, mental cases and psychos who pass through daily.

I flicked the cig to the pavement; ambers bounced along the ground and faded out as fast as they were born. I decided to go to my truck and get my provisions into my room first before the walk across the street. Florescent tubes flickered above the motel overhangs in need of repair. The doors paint slightly peeled and scratched; reminders of how everything in this country is old like some museum, or an old faded memory of someone's grandparent.

I throw my duffle bag on the bed; put a couple bottles of J&B on the nightstand for later. I pull out a yellow legal pad from the bag along with a pen and set it down on the complementary desk. The room is generic, like any other you would find in the state: an afterthought. Many have passed through here: Whores, families, illegal immigrants, adulterers, writers, and maybe the occasional suicide.

The place feels heavy with debauchery; loneliness, echoes of previous trysts and smells of morning regret. Traditional pastel colors adorn the walls along with cheap paintings of times long ago on countryside's and beaches. This will do I thought.

Stepping out of #6 the humidity hits like a wall and I can hear what sounds like a woman's faint scream, some banging around followed by whimpers and moans. It sounded pretty rough; probably putting on a show for her friend in there. No street tail yells like that unless she wants more out of it. All I could think about was its almost too damn hot out here tonight for that type of fucking.

***

The moon hangs above the pub, and white lines of light stream through the one palm tree that stands beside the bars wooden sign that reads "The Leaky Drum" in thin neon tubes attached to the exterior. The interior when I walk in is typical of any biker bar or truckers paradise; men shaped like large bowling pins, aviators at night, the smell of leather and BBQ. Eddie Money's "Shakin" is mid way through its play when I entered.

Their leers [the bowling pins] tell me I am out of place for sure, but I couldn't give a fuck; I am hungry and spazzing for a drink like some starved hyena or meth addicted razor head. The barmaid, way past her serving prime, waddles over and takes my order: "The Brew House burger, a whiskey *neat*, and a Coors to wash it all down," I stressed.

I noticed the leers stopped after I purposefully announced my order with more bravado than necessary. Anything less or in the area of a salad or cranberry vodka would have gotten my ass kicked in the parking lot later, or at the very least, a drink over my head accompanied with some sort of derogatory slang. There are a lot of greasy motherfuckers in here. Most of them are transients, the really bad ones. The others are just fine and not much trouble if you know how to handle them. Shoot the shit with them about the mundane- work, the grind, evil Russia, where to score and how to find it.

I was never *like* these folks growing up, but it's easy to play the part. Just pretend you share a common disdain for anyone of color, sexual persuasion or anyone not "normal." Also, I try not to talk the way I think. Just try to talk as less as possible in general.

After a quick side step to the Liquor store to grab a couple more packs of Belmont and another Camel, I make my way back to the room. It's getting to be around 10:00 P.M. and I haven't even started on what I set out here for. As I make my way over, I can feel my belly full from that burger, and the slosh of the whiskey and Coors. As I realize that I may have ate too fast, the door of room #8 opens up abruptly; it's that girl again in the red heels. She is shoved outward and the door slams shut. She starts walking away towards the ice machine that's down a few holding what appears to be her nose. Curiosity struck me.

I lit one of my Camels out of its new package and stood by my truck, watching the pumps again and periodically at that girl at the ice machine. This girl hadn't been out here long; she looked to fresh from what I could tell, not a lot of mileage on her odometer. She wouldn't last out here too long though; she almost look's *too* good for this type of shit.

My thoughts are interrupted as I notice the red heeled vixen slowly making her way back over towards #8, stops a bit, looks in my direction and continues over closer. Her heels clicking like that state troopers did against the concrete, the florescent tubes above the overhang provided just enough light to make out her figure and face; her hips outlined by the almost painted on skirt, black in color. Her Heels matched the color of the almost dried up blood I could make out on her face, a face with good symmetry.

She stared through me like a thousand yards as she walked up, gave me one of those slutty looks but her voice and tone almost had a false sense of bravery. She pulled out a cig of her own.

"Got a light there stud?" she said flirtatiously. I got closer to her and gave her a light. Her eyes are wide, and blue in color; with a little too much liner that's beginning to run from the nights work, a smell of citrus came off her body, sweet but faint, along with the musk of a man.

"What's your name cowboy" She said with a slight flirt.

"You go first darling, beauty before age where I come from."

"My names Holly," she said after she took a long drag from her cig, while blowing the toxic smoke at some moth that seemed to be attracted to her. "Well, mines Cobb. Been a rough night?" Pointing to my nose but referring to hers; it still being a tad bloody. She wiped it a bit with the ice cube in her hand, making the cube change to a reddish hue. "Is it fine if I call you Cowboy since you got them fancy boots on and all?"

"Sure, if you must." I sighed. She took a puff and blew some out the side of her mouth, the smoke rolling over her lips like fog over a valley.

"You know how it is Cowboy, these guys ain't the most charming. Say... you think I can come in and borro--." I stopped her mid sentence; I knew what she was getting at. A girl like her just doesn't ask for things without any string attached.

"Hold a sec here, and be honest with me... Holly. Your Para-Trooping tonight correct, you ain't gotta place to stay, am I right?

She paused for minute, took another drag as if to stall and think carefully about her answer. I tried not to stare at her figure but couldn't help it much; her breasts pushed up high in her tightly fitted tank top, that cherry blossom lipstick I could now distinguish from the lights above. She noticed this.

"Look handsome; I'll be true with you. I *would* like to come in if I can and wipe my face down and maybe even freshen up in the shower. I promise I will make it worth your while Cowboy, no charge for you stud."She said as she moved close up on me while reaching near my crotch but tugging up on the lanyard. I could feel a buzz down below, a slight rise in the atmosphere beneath my denim.

"It's *not* gonna be like that Holly. You come in quick, take your shower, freshen' up and then you're out," I stressed while taking her hand away slowly from the lanyard, my crotch.

"Gee man, never had a guy round these parts say something like that to me. No disrespect or nothing. Ya married or something, Gay?"

"No. Just didn't come up here for that kind of evening"

"Hmm..., It just seems weird in all me being honest, a solo guy like you up here not to party and all."

"Just get in the room and take the shower," I said with hint of annoyance now.

The J&B was warm on my tongue while I sat at the desk staring at the yellow legal pad in front of me. Holly was in the shower and throughout the duration she intermittently hummed a tune which sounded like that new Kim Carnes song. A few moments later, the shower turned off and the door opened a quarter. I looked briefly but couldn't make out her figure. Holly was still fixing up behind the door and I refocused my attention back to the J&B and the desk. Soon I could hear the door open fully and could feel how hot that shower was, the warmth of the steam rolled into the air conditioned room invading its space. I could hear Holly mess about behind me, and her little footsteps towards my desk on the green shag beneath. "Pour a lady a drink too handsome?" She questioned in a playfully coy voice.

When I turned around she was no further than a few feet. Her small mound in full view through her panties right at eye level, beads of water not dried from the shower showed small wet spots beneath its surface, her tank top the same. Her pale skin seemed more tanned with the yellow light in the room.

It's difficult not to stare when a woman pulls this stunt. You get those old feelings like when you were in junior high: that first rush of primeval ecstasy from a first kiss, or when you got a peep-show from the school skank after the bell behind the bleachers; or even a blowjob if she were so obliged.

Girls learn from an early age how to manipulate men. They start it with their fathers, and then continue with their boyfriends and lovers. Boys learn from an early age how to lie, first to their mothers who birthed them, then to their girlfriends and wives. It just depends on what the other wants.

"How old are you? You probably ain't even old enough for a drink girl," I said bluntly. "Put the rest of your clothes on too, I told you no funny shit. I am not playing games."

Her face turned to slight disappointment but kept a hint of playfulness.

"Easy there cowboy, there's no need to be edgy. It's just hot in here now but I'll put my skirt back on if you'd like it. Plus you ain't supposed to ask a girl that question, it ain't polite." she said as she picked up her skirt and wiggled her way teasingly into it. I pretended not to notice this.

"Yeah, sure," I snuffed.

"By the way Cobb, I am old enough to do a lot of things as you have probably figured out," she said in a snarky tone almost toying with my questions. She came closer again and looked over my shoulder. "What are you some writer or something, come here to write about Valdosta and its shitty rest areas?" she added mockingly.

"If I were to tell you, would you leave?"

"Maybe...What's your deal anyway Cobb, why don't you want to have a go at me? I was thinking about it in the shower and couldn't shake why you just don't take me like the rest," she said in an almost insecure way, pouting her lips as she now moved onto the bed, her legs crossed but I could still see slightly up her skirt, the blue peaking through, teasing my thought process.

A large part of me wanted her, wanted to feel what she was all about but she was old enough to be my daughter if I had one, and I was raised different. I am not sure that's something a girl like this could fully understand with being in this life and all; bikers, lonely truckers, transients of all kinds with no qualms about how it affects everything: the nation's heartbeat.

"I'm sorry; I didn't mean to cause a scene. I just ask a lot of questions and pry when I am nervous, that's all" she added, feeling slightly out of line for whatever reason.

"What are you nervous about?

"Me?" I said.

"No, it's because you were right Cowboy; I don't have a place to go tonight. That guy you saw push me out a while ago, I thought he would be my roof, ya know, for the night.

"Thought that if you waved your cat all in my face the way you did outside and after your shower just now you could stay here tonight, right?" I said in a mocking tone.

She paused and carefully thought about her answer; her look was different than her recent attitude from before.

"Yes. That's the truth, honest."

Finally this girl showed me some honesty, it was refreshing. A small part of me was now actually enjoying her company even though her voice, her body and sexual energy, was a major distraction. It's a rare occurrence though in these parts to get real honesty out of someone with all the masks, acting and hypercritical performances you see on a daily basis. This made me curious, and I decided to break my rule in what I had said before.

"I tell you what, Holly. You can stay here tonight. No booze though and still no funny business. Just be honest with me and you can stay. That's all I ask."

"Really Cobb!?" She said in a surge of surprise as she perked up a bit in her posture.

"Yes."

"Thanks a bunch! But what are we going to do the whole time?"

"Well, I am going to sit here, think (drink) and you can ohh...I dunno, watch TV or go to bed. How's that sound?" She was bored already, "Can we talk Cowboy? I haven't really *talked* to anyone in a while," She said in allusion to her lifestyle. "We *are* now aren't we?" I said as a matter of fact while I poured myself another glass of J&B into one of the motel's glasses.

I could see Holly thinking up a storm in her little head as she re-crossed her legs yet again, touching her hair with two fingers in a stroking fashion; looking for spilt ends."What does paratrooping mean Cowboy...?"

"Like what you said earlier outside." She added.

I kicked off my boots that still remained on my feet since we entered, wiped a bit at my brow and took a deep sip of my drink before answering.

"It's just an expression. During WWII American paratroopers who were apart of the D-Day land invasion would parachute from planes behind enemy lines. The Nazis at the time occupied the Netherlands, France and so on and so forth. During the night was when most Allied paratroops' would happen to fall from the skies, and they would seek refuge within the small villages and towns that were not strategically important enough to keep Germans in at the time." I stopped.

"You follow so far?"

"Yeppers, keep going Cobb. My ears are even faster than some of these guys out here."

"Right. So the village people would see the Allied soldiers, them being liberators, and would secretly house them and put them up for a brief period giving them food, shelter and what not. In the modern sense of the phrase I meant it as you were seducing me for a place to stay for the night, banging for roof or paratrooping as it were."

She motioned to the window with a nod, "Well it's like a battlefield of some sorts out there ya know Cowboy, people and all." I stared out between the drapes that cover half the window, the light from the moon cascading over the dilapidated structures, the broken road, the chipping paint of the poles and signs.

"Yeah, you're right in an odd way" I said in surprised agreement. Holly looked back at me as she made circles with her finger around her knee. "So, in a way you are like a Frenchman giving me shelter from all the bad Nazis out there, and I am your liberator? I guess we are both White Knights in a way, people who try to help others huh."

I paused for a moment before affirming her.

I was shocked at how dumb this girl had led herself on to be. An actual glimpse of intelligence came through her words, her understanding in her application. What gives? It made me even more curious, and slightly uncomfortable. I looked at her slowly before asking, her eyes watching me and studying and anticipating the conversations direction.

"Be honest with me again Holly, why are you here doing this. Do you have a family somewhere? What's your deal?" She reshuffled herself on the bed before counter offering.

"Tell me about the yellow paper, the J&B and you got a deal Cowboy." I thought about her proposition, non-sexual in nature; a surprise.

"You're alright Cowboy, I like talking to you. I feel like you are actually listening to me. I knew you were different when you gave me that wink after I got off that rig out there earlier," she added before I could get out my answer.

"Fine, it's a deal." I broke another rule just then. I poured Holly a small drink. Walked up to her on the bed and handed it to her then shuffled back to my chair, slightly feeling a buzz coming on. Her citrus scent had turned to the smell of the motel shampoo; a strong lavender. Though be it cheap stuff and all, it still managed to smell good on her. She gladly took the glass of J&B but didn't question my action. She knew it was a gesture of conformity; a social formality when bonding.

For some guys, booze will make the urge to fuck increase. For me at least, it seems to dull those urges even though they are still present beneath the numbness. It's amazing to me anyway; in America you can drive, get married, go to war and fuck before you can even drink. Some rules are just absurd.

Holly sat up on the bed, legs folded underneath her now, sipping her drink and then resting it with her hands back down on her skirt between her thighs. I sat looking up into the ceiling, about to go into thought and conversation about what I am doing up here.

The ceiling was white popcorn; two water stains appeared in the one of the corners near the wash-room. The dim yellow lighting casting shadows over the floor and on the furniture from the one lamp by the bed. "I had a wife; it's been about a year now." I said almost too abruptly without any emotion.
"Divorced? She cheat on you stud?"
"No. Killed"

"Oh... shit Cowboy, I'm sorry. Is that why you drink much and up here tonight?" She asked still puzzled. "I always drank, not like my old man, but been taken to the bottle more frequent now." I sniffed while taking another sip of my drink; Holly did the same with hers but coughed slightly as she took it too fast.

"She was expecting our first child. On the way home from her moms house, who lived in Ocala, there was a bank robbery in Gainesville. The thieves fled south down I-75, cops in full chase, shots being fired and all. At one point they crossed the median into the northbound lane, it was rush hour and traffic was heavy. They hit her, spun out and rolled their van. It was head on, there was nothing anyone could do."

Holly was stunned and didn't know how to respond. She just nodded and looked sad and took another sip of her J&B. I continued.
"Those men, those thieves...they were pieces of *shit* Holly, a real skid-mark on the underpants of society"

A part of me wanted to scream. Who could care though, Holly? She's got her own issues. Who was to blame really? This is what happens when a nation has begun its slow circle of the drain- the people turn on each other, they steal from one another when less is no longer more. *More* becomes the void to which all want to fill. Greed is the vacuum to which consumes us all until there is nothing left to chew on.

Holly could probably tell the memories were making me uncomfortable in the way I was taking big swigs. I tried to hide it but that sort of thing can show easy on a person, even with the devil's juice is coursing through the veins. I quickly changed the direction of topic.

"So anyway, I came up here because I am lost at the moment. My ranch is about to be foreclosed on by the government and I have no direction. A friend of sorts (a small lie) told me the best thing to do would be to take the "legal pad trip."

"That's a thing?" she asked, as If I were some old loony making up stories through the bottle.

"Sure. What you do is when you are lost in the world you book a room somewhere, a few hours or so from home. Go by yourself of course, and bring with you just a yellow legal pad and something to write with. You write down all about who you think you are and what you want to be. Write down your strengths and what you as a person can improve on. Write down what you don't like about yourself, what others might not like about you."

"That sounds easy Cowboy, how come you ain't got anything down? You seem to know a lot, smart and all." She said while taking note of the few drops of J&B she had manage to spill on her top.

"Well, the hard part about it is you have to be honest with yourself." I said as I looked at her and then towards the old pictures of the beach and countryside on the wall.

"Anyways, I've said too much. It's your turn."

Holly then pulled her legs out from beneath and straightened up on the bed, fidgeting with her drink, slightly nervous. I could tell she wasn't used to this sort of introspective conversation.

"There's no reason to feel sorry for me Cobb, I had a good life. I mean I had everything done for me and taken care of. My family has money and all, just never the time." She touched her hair again in an insecure way, trying to regain a sense of power and control. A woman will do this when she feels powerless.

"No one really paid much attention though to me. I got into the wrong crowed at school, started doing drugs and boys. The only time my dad really cared was when I had a pregnancy scare. Other than that he works all the time, that's all he cares about."

"So you pull tricks out here because daddy didn't read you stories at night, that's it?" I said slightly mocking her. She took it lightly because she knew it was absurd.

"I know what you're thinking Cobb. Oh poor rich girl, daddy doesn't pay attention blah blah blah." She phrased while making hand gestures as if speaking through them. "I know it's stupid and I didn't want to end up here... it's just... I didn't want to become like them, boring and all ya know."

"Plain Jane." I said.

"Yeah exactly, I wanted adventure, something different, something not what everyone else has...."

I thought about what she had said just then and realized again how small the room was or had gotten. "Why don't you do something with singing, go to Nashville or some shit? I heard you in the shower earlier, you have the voice Holly." She seemed flattered by this comment, her voice soften up.

"Maybe that's what I should figure out, I've always want to sing or write songs. I used to have a book at home where I would write stuff down in, lyrics, poems that sort of thing ya' know?" She said with her drink now empty. Motioning to me for another pour but I didn't. Her body was starting to get loose again, her gaze going back on auto pilot towards seduction; her legs now slightly out of alignment, showing more than they should again. I began to smell the exotic tang from her again.

"I think that will be all tonight."

"Yeah, I think your right Cowboy. I am quite tired now too." She sighed as she motioned for me to take the glass away from her hand, tipping from side to side. "Honesty will do that to you." I said while taking the glass from her hand noticing the color of her nails just now, a deep purple, a few of them weathered and fading like the paint outside. "You can have the bed; I will sleep in the chair over here." I said in contradiction to my body's signals.

"You *sure* about that decision Cowboy?" She said, waving her finger in a come hither motion at me as she crawled onto the bed, ass slightly up and back ached as if she was presenting like some sort of primate. I could feel that buzzing beneath the numbness again, that primordial energy.

"Don't you go start again with *that* now." I said as she laughed as she gave a teasing look

"I *know* stud, just kidding around and all this time."

Thoughts of the bowling pins I saw earlier in that pub started spiralling in my head, the truckers at those pumps out there; the girls stepping down from their cabs. My stomach feeling knotted and heavy as if concrete had been poured down my throat. Holly's former evening escapades with those transients, the spreading of effluence and the toxicity in the air.

How different would I be if I acted with Holly? I would be just like the rest of them, the same, just like any other John who got his load off in her. I wanted to be different in some way. These thoughts made me nauseous, the J&B. I sat back in my chair. Holly went under the covers. I drifted in and out of thoughts, the legal pad sat idle in front of me.

When I woke up, I accidentally hit the glass over on the desk with my arm, spilling the backwash left in it. I looked at the clock on the night table, 3:30 am. The light was still on and I got up to turn it off. The clicking of the switch caused Holly to wake in her stupor. I could make out her toned and hour-glass figure in the bed slightly, me hovering over the edge.

"Cobb come sleep here with me. I promise I won't try anything. I just want you to sleep with me." Her phrasing confused my inner vocabulary of what everything meant, the words she chose and the way she used them.

I crawled in bed with her and laid there. I could feel her move around as she scooted her ass a bit towards my body, almost as if to just get closer to my energy. The yellow legal pad sat blank on the desk.

***

Warm light burned through the discounted drapes in the room waking me from my stupor. Holly was still fast asleep, the bed sheet between her legs and thighs as if she wanted something there to be close and pressing; her blue panties now riding slightly up her ass due to midnight shuffling and made the tightness of her checks more noticeable in the morning light. I didn't wake her. I packed my things slowly and carefully, dumping out the rest of the booze in the sink. Before checking out I left her a message on a piece of yellow legal pad and left it on the desk.

Holly, you should find a bit of money on the night stand next to your clothes. It's not much ($50) but use it well. Get a room for yourself and your own legal pad. Leave this place, this life. Find what you are looking for, the answers are always with us.

Cobb

On the drive back to Gainesville I thought back about how odd the night was, the way the events transpired and why they happened that way. The urges, the honesty, and the contradictions between what my body wanted and what my mind didn't. I didn't write down anything. Had my trip accomplished anything? What would I tell my therapist? Certainly not the truth, therapy is embarrassing enough for a man.

When I got into town it was bustling, it was a nice day out for the activity that I saw; dogs being walked, kids on the playgrounds, mothers shopping and picking their sons and daughters up from school. When I got to Dr. Pringle's office it was mid-afternoon, one of his receptionists, a tall thin waif-like brunette had me sit in the waiting room for sometime as he was late finishing up lunch. The news headline on CNN on the office TV read:

CNN Breaking News: Dow Jones Index closes above the 2,500 mark for the first time.

A drop in the ocean, for now I thought, even though the stock market isn't anywhere close to the true representation of the economy at large. This country is a patient that has a terminal illness, bound to be on life support for the rest of its days until the final pull of the cord. Symptoms abound, a slow decay from within; the host will devour itself unknowingly. Before continuing another inner ramble, a different receptionist, blonde one this time with a thick waist, called me in for my appointment.

His office was bright today. Windows opened and light from the hot Florida sun rippled in onto the rich mahogany surfaces, bouncing off desk ornaments, golf trophies and mementos from clients of past. Pictures of family and friends were on the side wall; further garnished this holiest of lavish spaces. We talked small chat for a bit just to ease into it. I sat in the black leather chair in front of his desk this time though, I intend this session to be quick since I didn't have much to report.

"I'll be honest doc, I didn't quite do what ya asked me to do." I said almost sheepishly, but I caught myself quickly and adjusted my posture. "I mean, I did, but I don't have anything written down. I guess I discovered things I already knew about, like the answers were always there." I tossed the blank legal pad onto his desk looking away from him almost embarrassed that I couldn't do such a simple task. He looked at me a moment, his designer glasses slid down his nose slightly as he pulled them back up to his bridge. He picked up the legal pad.

"I see that Mr. Cobb, but, there IS a page missing though" He said inquisitively but in a non judgmental tone.

"Well yes, I mean, I did write something down but it wasn't for me." But before I could expand on that thought I noticed a picture slightly turned on his desk in front of him, it was the only picture he had on there, the rest were on the wall. I could make out that it was a girl, a daughter perhaps. "That your daughter there doc?" I said in a calm demeanour.

He paused for a minute, almost in deep thought; memories swirling around. I could tell something about my prying triggered something inside of him; it wasn't anger, but a sort of sadness that draped across his face for a moment before he handed the frame to me.

"Yes Mr. Cobb. That's my little girl. Frankly I haven't seen her in a while. She left our place a while ago, and her 19th birthday just passed. There was a falling out of sorts. She's been gone a year now." He said with a tiring look and hopeless tone. I grabbed the frame. Those eyes were familiar, that figure burned into my brain; those lips and that innocent yet rebellious glare.

"Do you mind me sir asking what her name is" I said, almost feeling like a rookie detective who had just solved his first case. He then breathed out the name I had foreshadowed in my matrix of thought and intuition.

"It's my Holly. Why do you care Mr. Cobb?"

"Because I just realized I found something in Valdosta after all Doc."

"Oh yeah, and what's that?" he said in a now interested manner.

"That it's a smaller world than we think."

***

There was a day as a kid when my school took us to the Science Centre in Orlando. I remember wandering off from the group and stumbling upon a room that showed how cancer spread in time lapse inside of a lab animal. The images were raw, disgusting and have reverberated in my mind since then.

The cells in the body constantly 'talk' to one another, ensuring that they are doing the right things at the right time to keep the host healthy. Most normal cells in body tissues stay put, stuck to each other and their surroundings. Unless they are attached to something, they cannot grow and multiply. If they become detached from their neighbours, they commit suicide. But in cancer cells the normal self-destruct instructions do not work, and they can grow and multiply without being attached to anything, causing a deadly imbalance to the system and its host.

If you love anything in this world, you better hang on to it tight tooth and nail.

A wolf is always at the door.

SPOTTING TRAINS

Oakland County, Michigan 2010

They say when you hit thirty all anyone mentions to you is how they wished to be that young again and have the future still wide open. They are jealous because you haven't made any large mistakes like they have yet and that you still have a chance to carry out your dream vision of what you desire out of this existence we call human life, a waking life.

Jake has vowed to stop listening to the voice inside of his head, along with the medley of other people's opinions about how he should get his life in order and what his path should be as a father, husband, and Weather Man. Thirty-years of listening to the voices of others has gotten him nowhere in his quest and vision for the life that he once dreamed for himself; a life of adventure, opportunity and creation. Instead, Jake has a good life, an average life.

It is a humble one in existence to which no one could complain. So why is it that he carries a weight around so heavy that it is so painful as to wake up every morning, look himself in the mirror and ask himself the same questions day in and day out *"Is this what our lives are suppose to be,* and *how did we know we would end up like this?"*

Too much pressure and too many demands, long hours for little to no money, no time for family and no time for people; life in modern day America is high demand, low yield. Everything is too expensive, yet everything is disposable, just like people. No appreciation for core ethics/values. Hyper materialized, over sexualized, desensitized, and violent. The modern day life package is a poor investment and risky venture.

The uncontrollable urge to listen to others comes from Jake's ritualistic nature of heading to the tavern by his studio every day after work to stare into the abyss of his golden colored IPA. People tell Jake everything: plans after retirement, cheating on their spouses with childhood crushes, fears of a nuclear Iran and how Xbox is better than Play Station. People tell him the truth and vice versa because the truth comes out while consuming large quantities of alcohol; especially with people to whom we have no immediate connection to. Also, the fact that bars and clubs play music gives people the feeling of anonymity and thus perpetuates conversation towards the hidden and scandalous.

Jake sees himself as somewhat of an archive for people's most inner thoughts and stories. It doesn't matter if some of them are lies and hyperbole; it just makes him feel better knowing that someone's day, or life for that matter, is perhaps worse than his at the moment. He secretly wishes though that someday at the tavern the man who he saw banging his wife right before he jumped out of their two-story apartment window would come in and confess this to him; so as to thank him instead of wanting to break his nose and send him into a dark coma.

He would not only thank him, but also buy him a drink for freeing him from a life that he never wanted and wife he never really loved. Marriages today last around 11.3 years on average, so Jake has found some relief in these statistics he saw yesterday in a Huffington Post article; a relief that he isn't the only loser in the bar today at noon.

Jake's past life was a lie and he still carries half of it with him every day he goes to work. Being a Weather Man (a meteorologist) is the only job in the world where you could be wrong every single day and not get fired for it. You could lie and say that a Hurricane is about to hit the United Kingdom and pass it off as a misjudgement in the weather models.

Jake also knows that his station has it out for him since they keep hinting to him that they want to re-tool and start with a fresh look to keep viewers interested in the weather news. *How is this possible?* Jake always asks. It's weather after all, and the only time people pay attention is if it is going to severely impact their time and path towards the nearest retail outlet, trendy restaurant or latest gizmo at Radio Shack.

Jake knows exactly what they are going to do to him; they are starting to bring in young and gorgeous looking "weather girls" to spice things up. Jake couldn't care less though; he knows that this is what networks do in desperate times. It's all about capturing eyeballs, not about content.

They always bring in attractive individuals because it has been proven in many studies that people tend to believe and pay more attention to beautiful people, even if what they are saying has no merit whatsoever. This is what really bothers Jake. Everything in his life is broken beyond repair, everything is staged from the rat-race to the news he sees on the T.V. screen.

Jake is finding that bachelor life is harder now than it was when he was in his late teens and twenty-something's. Not because he has been out of the game for a while now, but because of how life has changed Jake to this very moment. Women are looking for different things now at his age instead of cocky-wit, and few good dance moves before the call for a cab to his apartment is made.

It's all about stability at his age and if he can provide a possible future for all the desperate divorceés or marriage hopefuls looking to get hitched in hopes of not becoming a crazy animal lover that reeks of cat-piss and yells at passerby's out their bedroom window during lonely Saturday nights.

Society now shames Jake if he stray's away from the programming- going after, or dating young women who are attracted to Jake's status would result in social shaming. People would tell him to "man up," or claim that he needs to start acting like an adult and continue along the conveyer belt of social responsibility, when in fact Jakes biology is saying otherwise. Jake as a man is only beginning to enter his prime, men age differently from their counterpart's of course.

It's tough for Jake now even more so that his finances are crumbling faster than a Janga tower. The rosacea that powders Jake's cheeks is an early indication as to why he has very little funds. He drank away most of his savings along with any visitation rights to his only child and all that he has to show for now is what looks like a mishap at a tanning salon, and a melancholic aura that seems to repel the ladies who might have been interested in him like cheap cologne from Hollister. It also doesn't help when the alimony payments are breathing down Jake's neck like an irate CEO before an earnings quarter.

Secretly though, Jake is in love with his next door neighbour, Stacy. They have never really talked or shared a brief smile or "Hi there!" She is single from what he can tell by his daily stalker-esq tendencies that borderline on obsessive, even something a mid-rank P.I would be proud of.

Jake doesn't see himself as one to be "that" way though, he doesn't think of his voyeurism as something of a perversion because he too has seen her glance at him through her kitchen window while he has been doing yard-work. He wants to somehow get to know her better, but this isn't customary anymore in today's society. Jake has been noticing that people are becoming increasingly socially afraid and awkward, and are only interested in human contact if it somehow directly serves their life. *It's like the world is on auto-pilot, but who is still pressing the buttons?*

People in subdivisions don't do such things. The only time neighbors come out and talk to one another is if the power goes out or when shovelling their driveway. Would she even want to get to know him?

She seems like the type of woman that doesn't need anyone or want a man in her life, yet when she stares there is always a brief hope that she does. Why do we deny ourselves now, why do we lie to our human nature to which laughs at us every time we pretend? Who am I kidding though, she has been witness to my former married life, my previous fights with my ex-wife and the nights where I would just sit and chain-smoke on the porch while drinking out one of our wine bottles from our wedding day.

These are the thoughts that constantly paralyze Jake from acting towards his curious impulses towards his neighbor. He wishes sometimes that he could travel back in time so that he could move into the neighborhood before he married too young and had a kid. Maybe then, his lust, love or whatever this was could happen. He wonders if she was ever married or has a kid or does she not believe in such things, maybe this could be something they'd have in common. Jake will never know though because he keeps listening to that inner monologue in his head that stops him from ever achieving happiness.

Oh well. Jake has tranquillity now. Kind of. However, sometimes Jake wonders why it is that we have to live inside the confinements of society for eighty-odd years of our existences and not for five minutes can we escape it and all of its tasks and bullshit. He also wonders why we have to wait until we die to escape the prisons of our bodies in order to experience the astral and the cosmos to which we all came from. We are after all made from ancient star dust.

When Jakes thoughts start to drift towards the Glock 17 in his bedside table like they have today, he takes a drive out to a place where he once visited as a child. Jake bought the Glock first as a means to protect himself against burglars, but he is too much of a chickenshit to actually use it. People like Jake in the event of a B&E would cower under the bed and beg for the police, browning their designer jeans all the while. Yet every night Jake fantasizes about French kissing that guns steely barrel- Ice cold metal on the lips, the scent of lead. Just one squeeze of the trigger and all the worlds' problems go away, along with Jake's. A lustful tango and romantic dance with mortality, yet Jake will never do it. He has no constitution for suicide; his will to live is strong for now and would rather guide him toward his neighbour.

The train station is out of service now, old and dilapidated; a relic of a time when people once frequently visited and left this town of his. It's still a place though where he comes to collect his thoughts. He used to come here with his mother as a child because he always wanted to spot the passenger and freight trains that sometimes passed through. He would rarely see any since the town wasn't on a major track into anywhere. When he did manage to see one though, he would always try and count how many rail cars where attached to the locomotive.

It was like magic to young Jake. *Where did they come from? Where are they going, and where is their final destination?* He always wondered when he was young if trains even cared where they were going and to what end. He wondered if they were conscious or had emotions. Now he wonders why our lives can't be like our train rides where we know exactly where we are going and what our final destination is going to be. Jake has always hated the fact that he has never known what his true path in life was, always searching but has never found the correct track, or if he has been on the right track for that matter. In a way though, passenger trains reflect a lot of what our lives are like.

Through life and on a train we get on and then someday we eventually have to get off whether we like it or not. Along the way there are many stops to which we will see strangers or even people we know that have to leave the train never to be seen again; it's the cycle of the train ride. However, new people replace the old as they get off the train and re-fill the seats once again, and the ride keeps going. New faces, more baggage and the same recycled conversations are once again seen and heard on the train ride. The thing for Jake, though, is what train does he want to get on? And where does he dream of going?

Suddenly, Jake spots a rare freight train passing through.

He begins to count.

THE SUBURBANITES I

Oakland County, Michigan 2010

S tacy is what you might call your "average" American girl. A now Suburbanite at heart, she is one of the many that sprawl into the urban jungle cul-du-sacs that canvass throughout the nation. Usually indigenous to America's Midwest.

She has big dreams for herself, including a long healthy life, a happy family, a supportive husband, a comfortable lifestyle, and hopefully to have some fun along the way.

Stacy has always been the do-gooder; the sensible one, the daughter any parent would be proud of. She went to Sunday mass every week with her parents, and volunteered at the community centre after school three times a week.

She got straight "A's" throughout high school, except in Geography class where she got a "B," was the captain of the school dance team, along with President of Student Council. She got accepted to all 20 colleges that she applied to, and had a really great experience at the one she finally chose.

Another shining example of the American Dream....

Stacy's favourite movie is *Leap Year*, a romantic comedy, like all generic rom-coms, that say to women that marriage is the end all and be all of life, and will fix all your problems as a person whilst making you whole, and that everything will be OK after the fact. Plus, getting married prevents being ostracized; by society, workforce pay raises, and especially by all your other married friends and family members.

It is the highest form of groupthink.

It's all extremely inspiring...and creepy, like some sort of cult.

However, Stacy had found that one guy that most girls will never have. It wasn't until her fourth year at law school when Stacy met her "true love", "the one,"

Bob. Un-renounced to her, she was set-up by a mutual friend (Robin) between the two of them who invited both her and Bob to a St. Patrick's Day Kegger. Stacy had always been the reserved one around men, the girl that always listened to her mom about them; and how all they wanted to do was to pick open that treasure box between her legs.

"If a lock can be opened by only one key, then it's a good lock. If a lock can be opened by many keys, then well...it's a pretty shitty lock," is what Stacy's mom always lectured to her. Basically telling Stacy to ignore her natural biological urges to mate with the best and most dominant out of the gene pool, and wait for some stable poindexter with a closet full of Dockers and a managerial job to support her and her presumed future offspring.

Nonetheless, there was something that separated Bob from the rest of all the Jagoffs Stacy came across during her campus prowling- something different, something solid, and maybe even a bit adventurous.

Bob made Stacy feel safe, comfortable, and relaxed about life and all the confusion that comes with being young and inexperienced. Above all, Bob could make Stacy laugh. The kind of laughter that makes you snort, and feel like Rose from *Titanic*, having you're insides crushed by a corset.

Bob and Stacy met by the keg at the party where Stacy accidentally spilled Bob's Pabst Blue Ribbon all over his leather jacket.

"Don't worry, it's just Pabst," Bob exclaimed over the loud speakers that were blaring. It's like spilling expensive water," he finished with a boyish smirk.

Stacy then caught herself giggling as if she were a teen who just saw her first dick on late night HBO. They then both began to share their thoughts on the party, along with their mutual disdain for shitty pedestrian beers.

It wasn't until Hey Jealousy by the Gin Blossoms started playing (Coincidentally both their favourite song) that Stacy starting feeling strange, in a good way. Was it the way Bob confidently put his hand on the small of her back? Was it his glimmering smile and boyish charm, the alcohol? Or the way in which music from our childhood instils a sense of familiarity and innocence? Regardless, Stacy had never felt such a sudden rush of cosmic electricity.

It was as if neon colour lights of ecstasy were running through her head, past her core, and escaping out through her fingers and toes.

After much dancing; and after one of Bob's quirky funny questions about if she ever thought Ric Ocasek from *The Cars* was an attractive guy, or if her mom's real name was Rachel, Stacy decided to do the opposite of what she normally did.

She decided, not only to roll her body onto Bob, but also the dice on life.

They both played roulette that evening. Not the kind you play at the fancy Casino with $15 Clamato Caesars off Figueroa and Sunset Boulevard, but rather the kind they played on Stacy's bed. It was a crisp spring night with a full moon, and like two sexually famished rabbits, the fevered frenzy on each other's bodies was over just as quick as it started.

Bob may not have been the marathon runner in the bedroom that night -more like a 100 m sprinter-, but Stacy didn't care.

It was all new to her, and oh so exciting.

Was it the new intense feelings from a concentrated dopamine release?

Or was it love?

Who really cares?

This isn't a lecture on human biology in an underfunded high school science class.

Either way, Stacy was happy, and couldn't imagine someone else making her feel this way. Stacy, after all those years, finally understood what that song Laid by James meant.

At that in itself, is priceless.

This week Stacy turned 27, her life is just getting started. She has so much to look forward to. Her and Bob just celebrated their fourth year of marriage; they now have two kids, a dog, a nice house with a white picket fence, and a tire swing in the front yard.

Recently, Stacy has just been hired at the new law firm (Hammershmitz & Atwood's) as a paralegal where she works long boring and tedious hours around testosterone fuelled Alpha males dressed in Vera Wang's finest.

Stacy will put up with the borderline harassment and warehouse comments by all the male Lawyers, for now.

After all, the pay is good.

More importantly, the benefits she receives will help with a second income to Bob's in order to support the ability to pay for the babysitting, new iphones, restaurant dinners, the trips to Tuscany and Carnival cruises that will never happen, their mortgage, and the gym memberships that will eventually go un-used.

After all, this is just stepping stone for Stacy's career- a notch on her business card, and the first step towards her dream of opening up her own law firm where she will specialize in family law and human rights cases.

Everything seems to be on track for Stacy... like a yuppie married *Erin Brockavich*.

What could possibly go wrong you ask?

Well, what Stacy doesn't understand, or see on the horizon, is that society today is designed to grind her down. For the first time in history we live in a world with constant stimulation, contradictory messages, and expectations.

Everything is go-go-go, rush here, do this and that; there is barley anytime for Stacy to just sit and think, let alone be by herself and take a look at her life to see if it is what she really wants.

Did she use her twenties to explore, try new things and understand herself as a person better? Was marrying young a mistake? Did she rush life before even beginning to live it for herself?

Stacy lives in an age where everything is done for her by technology, yet, life seems more complicated and confusing than ever before.

Advertisements from magazines off of Stacy's iphone tell her all her problems and flaws as a person, and how she should fix them. She lives in a society in which she can throw away things the moment they stop working for her, because she can just get a new version/upgrade: Consumerism of products and people.

Stacy and Bob still have the time though once a week to have their post Grey's Anatomy sex. It's not

anywhere near the level of an epic 80's guitar solo –
like something out of a Glass Tiger music video - it's
more like a generic top 40 pop song, that gets the
job done.

Of course, Bob and Stacy didn't see this coming.
It's not their fault that most of all the movies, T.V
shows, magazines and other mediums that they saw
forgot to mention the reality of this dream put before
them. Not even the parents of Bob and Stacy's
mentioned to them that it would be like this; as if it
were some sort of tribal secret amongst married
people not to discuss the 24/7 hostage situation that
takes place behind the scenes every day in their
homes.

*"Don't worry sweetie, it gets better with time,
promise,"* said her friend Robin (the one who set
them up).

As if trying to say that Stockholm syndrome will
soon set in at age 40.

Things don't get better for Bob and Stacy sadly....

Between Stacy working late all the time at
Hammershmitz & Atwood's, and Bob going on

business trips to Colorado to craft mission statements and do team building exercises (getting drunk and eating butter-chicken with co-workers), a void begins to manifest between Bob and Stacy.

The intimacy between the two of them slowly begins to fade like the colours on your favourite childhood shirt after years of it being put through the wash. And like most men in America, Bob starts to resort to internet porn and going to strip clubs; and thus develops an unhealthy addiction to the instant gratification that it provides.

Stacy begins to fill the emptiness with shoe shopping, *Jersey Shore* marathons, and pills of Zoloft to counter her own depression. However, she does take up gardening; as a sort of meditation and escape from the grind of her job, obligations, and her now virtually sexless marriage.

Anyways, one day while Bob is off for the weekend in Denver Colorado eating culturally diverse foods and crafting mission-statements, Stacey has been thinking about calling back that funny young waiter boy who served them at Denny's awhile back.

He'd slipped her his number on the back of the bill right under Bob's nose, saying that they were into similar kinds of gardening.

At first it seemed strange to Stacy that he would be the type of guy who would be into that sort of hobby. But really, he seemed to have good intentions, plus he was charmingly handsome and friendly.

Stacy called up her waiter boy friend after reading an article titled: 5 WAYS TO HAVE MIND BLOWING SEX WITH YOUR MAN in the latest Cosmo addition she picked up at Publix on her way out from the check-out counter.

She arrived at his place. They had a few laughs and a few drinks....

Things got a little playful, and the next thing you know Stacy is on her back (and various other positions she didn't know about) getting that awesome sex that Cosmo magazine was talking about from none other than, Mr. Denny's.

Somehow... it just happens.

This makes Stacy feel extremely guilty, and she is very distant from Bob when he gets off his evening Delta flight from Denver.

Bob then gets even more cranky and frustrated without his post-Grey's Anatomy Sex, which pushes Stacy more towards Mr. Denny's which causes her to keep getting that awesome rush and dopamine release along with the physical and emotional intimacy that Bob hasn't given Stacy in years since their first night together.

Was it the way Mr. Denny's reminded her of when Bob used to be that refreshing surprise? The man who made her laugh and feel wanted? Or was it because over time our bodies' chemicals and pheromones get accustomed to one another's causing a decrease in the sensations; like how an addict gets num to the very first high the moment he/she has experienced it. It can never be duplicated with that same drug anymore.

Who really knows? We are just observers of reality.

After the divorce, Bob and Stacy go their separate ways. And given the tilted balance of American divorce laws; Stacy gets the kids, the house, and half of Bob's salary to which he worked his whole life for.

If Bob only understood that in today's society getting married is the equivalent of walking into a casino: putting your house, half your salary, the kids, and any shred of dignity all on red; and spinning.

Oopsy daisy.

Stacy will never admit to her friends, family or Bob for that matter, that some days she will just drive around aimlessly through the city listening to the Gin Blossoms on repeat, thinking to herself,

"We're we meant to live like this?"

"Is this even natural what we are doing to ourselves?"

Then suddenly, the song New Solution by Shirock blasted over her radio. And everything then just made sense: An epiphany of the highest order. She felt that feeling she had long ago, that electric neon ecstasy running through her.

Was it because the song by Shirock is an Anthemic and ear-gasmic masterpiece?

Or was it because for the first time in her life, Stacy, just had an original thought; a thought of her own.

Stacy, like most her generation, were taught that when they were young and afraid at night, it was best to just close their eyes until the monsters went away. If only she was taught to face those monsters as soon as they emerged from her closet, then maybe, just maybe, her and Bob could have had a chance. If only they had the time, the energy and the courage to communicate to each other what was wrong instead of closing their eyes.

Oh well, at least Bob and Stacy will always have the Gin Blossoms to brighten up their days.

THE SUBURBANITES II

Oakland County, Michigan 2010

Bob is what you might call your "average" American. He pretends to have lots of money, but is actually broke or in severe amounts of credit card debt after spending it all trying to impress his friends- all of which include his elementary/high school classmates from 15-20 years ago.

He has big dreams for himself, including a long healthy life, a happy family, a loving wife, a comfortable retirement, and hopefully to have some fun along the way.

Bob has always been a really rock-solid guy. He had a paper route when he was 12 years old that made him over hundred and fifty dollars a week. He got straight "A's" across the board in school, except in French class where he got a "B". He applied to a good college and got accepted and had a really great experience.

Another shining example of the American Dream...

Bob's favorite movie is Forrest Gump, a story about how by having a solid set of core values, pulling yourself up by your bootstraps, and being a contributing member of society you can experience the best of everything western society has to offer.

It's extremely inspiring...

This week Bob turned 30. His life is really just getting started. He has so much to look forward to. Recently he's just been hired into a Fortune 500 company where he's got all sorts of cool perks like culturally diverse cafeterias where he can get egg rolls and butter-chicken in the same meal, or company getaways to Colorado where they do team building exercises and come up with mission-statements focusing everyone in on their goals.

Everything seems to be on track. You know.... like one of those Rockwell styled TV commercials that you see day in and day out on the tube.

How could anything possibly go wrong?

Well, there are a few things on the horizon that Bob hasn't seen coming. This is the stuff that didn't really get covered in University or even in Forrest Gump. First off, like most good Westerner's, Bob likes to eat "three square meals a day" at, restaurants like McDonalds and Denny's, where he loves to get the "Grand Slam" or the "Lumber Jack Special", combined with sitting in an office all day, causes Bob to get fat.

Bob has no idea that you're supposed to eat 6 small meals a day. Heck, Bob doesn't even know what a "macro-nutrient ratio" is, let alone that the largest meal of the day is supposed to be eaten at breakfast and not before bed. What Bob also doesn't know is that marketing companies blatantly lie to you. There are more gyms, diets, and non-fat foods available in America never before seen in its history, yet America is the fattest country on earth with 68% of its population considered fat or obese.

Why is this?

It's because America loves a good enemy. And every time America declares war on something, it has the opposite effect. The 'War on Drugs,' 'War on Terror,' and now the 'War on Obesity'. When you manufacture foods with no fat, yet contain tons of sugar and carbohydrates, it is empty in nutrition and will cause you to eat even more. Your body is still starved and thus you will feel hungry all the time. Combine this with a modern indoor lifestyle and you have all those extra and empty calories piling up and not being used which the body has to store them in what are called fat cells.

Whenever there is plenty food/resources available, people will always consume more than their fair share. This is biology. Your primitive hindbrain wants you to pack on extra fat for the winter or incase of famine. In the modern world there are no famines anymore, no food shortages and no threats. We have moved from an agricultural based society to the cities. People have lost basic instincts and do not know how to properly take care of themselves. It's either pharmaceuticals or diets, nothing natural.

Of course, like most educated citizens Bob is far more concerned about the exotic diseases he reads about on CNN.com while he's procrastinating at work -- like Aids, terrorist Anthrax, and even the dreaded Bird Flu-- than to worry about the much less interesting possibility of eventually dying because he's simply overweight.

See, when you ask Bob how old he'll live to be he says "Probably 75 or 80". Secretly though, Bob thinks he'll live to be a hundred or even a hundred and three. He's just too modest to say it out loud.

It never occurs to him that while the average American man lives to his late 70s, most of them have physiques that aren't really worth living in past 40. And that if he doesn't proactively take on habits like lifting weights and eating properly that his knees and cardiovascular system won't even be able to muster a simple jog up his quaint American street.

In addition, Bob also has a big debt on his credit card and he's in several thousand over his head right now.

It's humorous, because when Bob got approved for his new credit card he felt so cool and adult being entrusted with the privilege of having credit. What he didn't realize, and what credit card companies bank on, is that studies consistently show that given credit, the vast majority of human beings will be inclined to exchange the intangible numbers in a computer for the tangible goods that they can hold in their hands.

By allowing himself to go into debt more than two weeks pay (at least for "stuff" as opposed to investments like property or education), Bob is basically setting a pattern that ensures he'll live with a lifetime of debt -Paying interest upon compounding interest, always pushing for a "life-style upgrade" over just paying down credit cards and living debt-free.

Bob just keeps forgetting that he lives in the most consumer-driven society in the history of the world -- a culture that is literally designed so that you can have a fist full of cash, blink, and find that it's all gone.

Where did it go? *"Uhhhh... You know... Stuff."*

Luckily Bob has big plans...

Someday, who knows when but sooner or later, Bob plans to start a really cool business where he's going to make the cheddar biscuits. He knows, after all, that he's a really creative guy because all his friends tell him that he has the most awesome My-Space.

Sadly, Bob has been spending most of his time outside work reading Maxim Magazine and downloading Top 40 Radio Hits and Ring-Tone Rap from iTunes. Bob doesn't really spend a lot of time reading the classics or challenging his mind anymore because he's always burnt out from being immersed in the business culture at his work.

Bob says he has always wanted to write a book, go mountain climbing, or grow his own garden but he will never in his life achieve these goals.

Why?

It's because people like Bob, and the other 80% of the population, lack action, and get too complacent due to negotiating with the current societal system. It's hard to be average, play it safe and expect to be *something* at the same time. You can't do both. You have to take risks. Bob has to choose one or the other. Sadly, he chose the path of average, and the one that everyone else chose. The easy path, and the path already walk on by many.

Conforming for any man in today's world should be a non-negotiable. It's tough though because the current societal make-up makes life too easy, and therefore, people automatically need not apply for greatness. Humans respond to incentives. There is no incentive to be great in Bob's world, the suburbs. The incentive is to be like, and to be liked by the same kind. People like Bob are afraid to be great, because most people will eventually come to despise him due to his success and their lack thereof. Bob would rather be liked by many then to be ostracized by the very people to which keep him down- so that they [the others] can feel comfortable in their own misery.

What Bob doesn't understand is that while he was born as an intelligent guy, intelligence, focus, and creativity are like muscles which have to be engaged and worked out on a steady basis.

The fact that he was a straight "A" student (other than in French, of course) is really no longer relevant

- and in the past five years he's become the mental-equivalent of the fat guy who keeps talking about how he used to be in the best shape "back in the day".

Well, that's too bad. Bob might not be about to become the next Donald Trump or Bill Gates.

Oh well...

However life really isn't all about the Benjamin's/cheddar points... and life isn't necessarily even about living a long time.

Life is ultimately about quality.

Bob knows that no matter what, he has what a lot of guys will never have. Bob has found his true love... his wife Stacey.

It was at a party back in college that Bob and Stacey first met. They had mutual friends and hit it off after Stacey accidentally spilt Bob's drink over by the keg.

"That's OK..." Bob told her as he helped to clean it up. Later that night they hooked up and they've been together ever since.

Life has been good for Bob and Stacey. In the past few years they've bought themselves a nice house with a white fence and a tire swing in the front yard, and had a couple of wonderful kids.

Bob has been working long hours at work to provide everything that Stacey could ever need. They still have sex once a week (after watching *Grey's Anatomy*), and while it might not be the Who's-Your-Daddy marathon it used to be, the fact of the matter is that they're still very much in love.

What Bob doesn't know however, is that while his cholesterol-clogged heart is pumping on overdrive as he thrusts aimlessly through his 4 and 1/2 minutes of sex to orgasm, Stacey is on her back imagining that muscular/charming cutie-pie Matthew McConaughey who she saw in the movie How To Lose A Guy in 10 Days and with his shirt off in US magazine.

Of course, Stacey loves Bob to death. But Stacey has needs. She's a woman, and she's a human being.

And Bob is just so...well. Bob.

Anyway, while Bob is off for the weekend in Denver Colorado eating butter-chicken and crafting mission-statements, Stacey has been thinking about calling back that funny waiter boy who served them at Denny's awhile back. He'd slipped her his number on the back of the bill right under Bob's nose, saying that they were into similar kinds of gardening.

It seems weird that he'd be the type of guy who would be into gardening, but really, he seemed to have good intentions and Stacey really wants to get some new plants to show to Bob when he gets back home. Stacey calls up her waiter-boy and he invites her over to his house. Unwillingly, and after a lot of humor from her waiter-boy, Stacey decides that it's no big deal to drop by. She arrives and they have a few laughs and a few drinks.

Things get a little playful and silly and next thing you know Stacey is on her back (and various other positions she never knew about) getting plowed by

Mr. Denny's. Somehow it just.... happens. This makes Stacey feel extremely guilty, and she's very distant from Bob when he gets back home.

Bob gets cranky without his weekly post-Grey's Anatomy roll-in-the-hay, which makes Stacey seek more attention from her waiter-boy, which causes her to continue on getting railed, and plowed in a way that Bob hasn't done to her in years.

Eventually Stacey can't take the lying and divorces Bob -- taking the two kids, the dog (did I mention they have a dog?), and half of Bob's Fortune 500 pension plan.

Woopsie daisy.

Bob has no idea that any of this could be his own fault, believing that he'd done everything for Stacey that a decent husband could ever do. He hates her and in court he indignantly calls her a "deceitful bitch" Without thinking this whole situation was somehow his fault too. Flash-forward another 2 decades and now Bob is alone at 50 years old, divorced, broke, fat, unhealthy, and a workaholic. He's got himself a new big juicy slice of the North American Dream.

Well, at least he can watch Forrest Gump to brighten up his day...

THE DALLAS PRIVATE DANCER

Dallas, Texas 2020

ATTENTION CONSUMERS: 3 DRINK MINIMUM commands the brief attention of all who enter this palace of pleasure. The only two things that grab awareness in this joint are the prices of everything-flesh and drink. The three drink minimum is a cover charge set in place to immediately suck money out of any man as soon as he feasts his eyes on the buffet of lust that is well stocked at anytime. Everything has a price in here, in this world and in this country. America is no longer a country, it's become a business. One giant Vegas strip. High hanging fruit, that masquerades as low.

The name is Alexis, however I am known around here as "Diamond," a name given to me by rite of passage into the sub-culture of stripper-hood. A strippers name is not chosen by her own will, it is given to her through the story of her life leading up to the moment she is hired. It's actually quite symbolic of the sisterhood that surrounds this place of business and worship by the gents who frequent it's circus of entertainment. It's like a birthright, an almost ancestral tradition among the workers of the oldest profession in the world; once your name has been given to you it is official, you are part of a secret sisterhood.

How I got the name "Diamond" goes back to when I was growing up in Arlington, Texas. As a young girl living in that city I wasn't your typical Texan sweetheart: caked on make-up, out-going, short shorts, MTV addict, boy-crazy, pop-culture adorer, dreams of a white picket fence garnished with a farm-boy as a husband. That was not me by a long shot. I was shy, mysteriously independent (one would say anti-social) and a bit of a tom-boy. I was made fun of constantly at school for my lack of conformity, my disgust for groupthink culture and my complete un-caring attitude toward being a true southern belle like the rest of my female "friends." It's not that I wasn't attractive or anything, on the contrary- I am extremely hot. All the guys in this club can attest to that for sure; just look or feel between their legs and I am sure you will have a clue as to what they are thinking about me.

I was always beautiful; I just never showed my goods or what I was made of back when I was a teenager. It was hidden, covered up like a great political scandal waiting to be exposed for all to see. It wasn't until I was around 19 when a friend of mine dared me to dance at "amateur night" at a strip joint in Houston while we were visiting friends who were on break from their studies.

My friends couldn't believe it when they saw it- that I was actually hot (and could dance for that matter). Granted, I put on the sexiest piece of clothing I could find, and did my make-up in a provocative, yet tasteful manner. They couldn't believe it to the point where they had to send pictures via twitter to everyone they knew and who knew me as well (pics or it didn't happen mentality). I get it though, even if my friends told everyone with their mouths they still wouldn't have believed them. So pictures it was, and I was shocked by the response. When I got home, my Facebook was full of messages from all the guys who had ever made fun of me in the past wanting to "catch up" with me and "go for a coffee sometime."

I wasn't naive for my age though, I knew that all they wanted to do was to bed me, now that they have seen me in an objectifying way. I was offered many "dates"- dinners, movies, jewelry, and booze- even in some cases I would be offered trips from guys who once only looked at me because I used to flip them off down the hall-way at school. However, there was one guy who stood out from all the rest. Not because he didn't want to have sex with me instantly in the back of his Ford Shelby GT500 (he did because that was his idea of a date), it was because of what he said to me before he tried to "knight" me with his sword. I asked him why he wanted me, why he asked me to meet him that night. His answer was "Alexis, you're a diamond in the rough. Guys would kill for you!" That`s the name (Diamond) the girls here at the XTC Dallas Cabaret gave me after giving them my life story; I like the name a lot, and wouldn`t change it if I could. It's me to a tee.

I never slept with any of those guys who threw money at me overtly, hoping to get a taste of something that they had now valued and wanted. I realized the power that I had over them now, all those years of torment and ridicule because I wasn't "girly enough," now has finally vanished with the wonderful magic of puberty, the right top, and the right pair of pants. Like in the world of private dancers, sleeping with a customer is something one shouldn't do. If you sleep with a customer, you have lost your advantage to get anything. When you sleep with him, he will get what he has wanted and he will have no more motivation to give you anything more. He will no longer come into the club and spend money on lap dances anymore. You may get a couple hundred to sleep with him, but you can get a lot more through table dances and gifts. You need to create the illusion that there is a possibility of sex. This will keep him trying to have you, and at the same time he will give you all sorts of things.

Too often, girls spend all their time on rich guys. Well here is a clue. Rich guys believe that you should pay attention to them because they are simply rich. Remember, that one poor guy with $40 in his pocket who is willing to spend it, is worth more than a roomful of rich customers that think they are too cool to pay you. It's better to focus on the less wealthy clients, especially the young guys just starting out in the rat race. Why? Poor customers probably have never gotten a lot of attention from hot babes so they are eager and feel lucky to be near you. They often have inferiority complexes and will over compensate by paying money for it. There is also this wonderful thing called "credit."

The guy I am grinding up on now for instance is a sophomore at UNT (University of North Texas). He told me so just a minute ago nervously; His name is Justin, I can tell it's his first time here or anywhere like this for that matter. He is a sweetheart, and a really nice guy from what it seems. However, he confessed to me that he is having trouble finding a girl around this area and hasn't had much success so far in college; or High School for that matter. He told me that the girls at college dismiss him at school and even at the local bars (it's probably because of his lack of confidence-also he is cute, but not hot). I told him that he should be patient.

Women his age are all over the place (both in mind and body) and only tend to go after the older, hotter popular guys that have a lot of value and status. Right now in his life he is on the bottom of the status chain (his twenties will be a rough ride for sure) but I told him that once he hits his thirties, and is well established, he will be swimming in so much pussy he won't know what to do with it. You don't have to be a professor of human interaction to understand this. The vast majority of young women want to sleep with 20% of the male population (Alpha's) and the 20% of the male population gets to sleep with 80% of the women who go after them: It's mating 101. This, then leaves the Beta males frustrated, and thus begins to overly compensate by trying to win girls by buying them gifts, taking them on dates and being suspiciously "nice" to them.

That's why I get to meet a lot of divorced men here because they found out that their wife cheated on them with a "bad boy" type, an Alpha. I told him that if he is just patient, works on himself (confidence through having life experiences) and his body, he will soon be the valuable one because by his thirties all the women that turned him down will be the desperate ones--- a mix of divorcées, biological time bombs and women who wasted their youth "having fun" and are now scrambling to conform and find a man out of fear of being ostracized. I see it all the time even though feminism has proclaimed otherwise to us as women.

There is a natural order of life that can't be re-written by any ideal notion. Biological hard-wiring is unbreakable and almost impossible to re-write because it is something that can't be changed by thoughts and grand delusions. Like I said, he is a sweetheart. I told him this lap dance was on me this time (something I rarely do); tonight is a different kind of night though for me, and I am in a giving mood.

Tonight is a special night among many things. It is ladies night for starters, which means women get in for free, and drinks are half price-along with any dances if they so choose. Most girls come here out of a dare by their girlfriends, or visit as a place to pre-drink before going to a club to pick-up. It's funny because there are plenty of willing guys here right now to pick-up if you wanted some action this evening; granted the lot here aren't exactly the "quality" or type they are looking for--the non-creepy horny and desperate for nude women type.

I once asked a girl who usually pre-drinks here what she expects to find in a club versus here. She laughed of course, but said something like how it wouldn't be her "doing," making the guy lust for her; that it would be the main "doing" of me and the rest of the dancers here. I told her that we had a lot in common when it comes to men and the nightlife style of living in a big city; Women may want to get laid, but their main priority is to have a good time, be looked at (not touched) by guys and get some free drinks. Women may go out to bounce around and have a night out with their ladies, but they also want to dress up in high heels and short skirts so that men can undress them with their eyes. You can argue that this isn't true, that some women really do just go out to have fun, but even if so, having men drool all over them is still a plus. Basically, regular women don't like the idea of a man being turned on for other reasons except for the ones given by their women-hood. Stripper-hood, whatever you want to call it, is constantly in a cold-war stand-off with women-hood for this reason.

Life fascinates me in the way that if you look close enough you can see the hidden parallels of fallacy to which we all like to escape into yet are similar. All labels really do is hide the real truth from those who wish to bury their heads into the sand like an ostrich. For instance, the two ladies that look like they just walked off the set of "Real House Wives of Atlanta" are no different from me; we are similar in a way. We both wear make-up to appear more attractive to the opposite sex. However, whereas they want to attract the most dominant man, I want to capture the attention of every man in the club tonight (as much money as possible). We both wear the clothing that we wear to bait men into whatever our agenda may be; a relationship, sex with an Alpha, attention, or free Appletinies at any hole in the wall bar here in Dallas. The only difference between us though is the way in which we operate.

I operate overtly, with me you know what you are getting yourself into (at least you should). I represent fantasy, an illusion that can be bought with a 3 drink minimum; and perhaps some 1's and 20's stuck in my bra or G- string. You know exactly what the score is when you are with me, "Diamond." I am looked down upon by those women that you see in the "real world," a world that is also full of its own illusions to which people seem to have a hard time understanding because it isn't overtly advertised with a neon sign. I am a threat to the "real world of women." I am competition for the wallets, and security that the beta males provide for them. You would be surprised at the amount of times a man's wife, girlfriend or lover has come storming into this place, fuming mad, about their partners "extracurricular activities." Yes, the main difference between me and the other women is that they dress too for other women, whereas I only dress for the men I am intent on servicing.

Women are indeed very capable of aggressing against others, especially women they perceive as rivals. Stigmatizing female promiscuity — a.k.a. slut-shaming — has often been blamed on men, who have an instinctual incentive to discourage their spouses from straying. But they also have a natural incentive to encourage other women to be promiscuous. Sex is ultimately coveted by men, however, in my experiences women limit access as a way of maintaining advantage in the negotiation of this resource.

 Women who make sex too readily available compromise the power-holding position of the group, which is why many women are particularly intolerant of women who are, or seem to be, promiscuous. Basically, I and women like me who dress like "sluts" in the world outside of stripping essentially are ruining the bargaining power of other women, and basically cheating the game of getting a guy to commit to them (whatever commitment means to you). That's why you always hear women talking trash behind their friends backs about how slutty they look because they know that they have lost the edge; leverage by way of showing just a bit more curve and flesh.

 This is why instantly gratifying things like porn and strippers are hated amongst the general female populous because they represent an illusion that real women can't compete with. I am an illusion that can't be competed with. "Diamond" isn't a real person but a persona. Just like the things I wear, the makeup I use, and what I do to get all dolled up and perfect for all the men tonight; it's all a performance and no different from the performances that go on in real life between the sexes. We are all "Players" in the game, both men and women. Once people understand what the "Game" is then we can all stop judging one another and enjoy things for what they are because things never change in life, just the context of them do. Why do you think people always say history repeats it's self? There is a natural order to life with natural laws to which we can't escape. We may think we have changed, but the only thing that has is how much better we have all become at fooling ourselves.

I feel like telling you these secrets because the real reason why this is such as special night tonight here at XTC is because tonight is my last dance, my last night as a private dancer for good. I made a decision (came to a realization) last year that I can`t and won`t be able to do this forever. Eventually some younger, tighter and hotter version of me will come in and take my limelight away from me. It`s O.K though, I am smart enough to know that this is how it is. Beauty is a diminishing asset, and time ultimately takes its toll on our bodies. I have tons of money though; I am set and have been saving for a long time. Not a lot of girls here do. Some do but not all. Some will use the money to put themselves through college or pay off some debts; others have had a rough life and choose to spend it on blow and bad decisions.

***

Filtered lights can disguise a lot, but when you're up close and personal with a customer, there's no hiding your butt dimples. Not that they care! But you do; especially when you're off duty at the beach actually trying to look hot in non-artificial lighting for real-life men. A homemade scrub with coconut oil, brown sugar, and coffee grounds applied to "problem areas" before showering several times per week (or before each shift) can help reduce the appearance of cellulite. Work the mixture into the skin and let it set for 10 minutes before rinsing off. Tanning also evens skin texture, and cult product Maui Babe Browning Lotion not only is the fastest and most flattering tanning product I've tried, but also lists coffee as an ingredient.

Another dirty little secret I will give you is that the most hated individual in the club is the girl who wears Sally Hansen Airbrush or scented lotion onstage, putting her coworkers' lives in danger on the regular. If you want to be silky soft for work but don't want to get knocked out when a bitch goes flying into the crowd attempting a Flying Showgirl minutes after your Body Butter'd butt greased up the pole, add a teaspoon or two of coconut oil to a bath and soak in it, then towel off as usual. Also, Collagen and hyaluronic acid are two of the usual suspects in most anti-aging skincare products. But did you know that there are supplements you can take that are more effective and work from the inside out?

During a trip to Japan, I became obsessed with the Japanese "beauty drinks" sold in every drugstore that contain collagen and hyaluronic acid as active ingredients. When I came back to work, I had the skin of a 17 year old minus the acne -- the fine lines around my eyes and mouth were noticeably reduced and my pores were smaller. You could argue that the newly acquired glow was due to 10 days of the Japanese diet, but I'm sort of a health freak in my normal life and consumed predominantly ramen and Asahi while I was away. These products aren't available in the US (at least not for cheap -- hence me stockpiling 30 of them in the airport) Bonus: It's good for your joints, which are no doubt aching from more abuse in a couple of months than some people could ever rack up in a lifetime.

Anyways, the tradition here at XTC is that on the night of your last, you get the final stage dance of the night. The ritual is that the song you get to dance to is that of "Gypsy" by Lady Gaga. The manager and DJ here don`t announce to the crowd that it is your last time here, however, if you are a regular you know damn well that when you hear that song at the end of the night that the girl up there on stage is dancing for freedom. You can tell who the regulars are too because they usually stand throughout the whole song and tip extremely well as to send you off on your future endeavors. Also, it is tradition that the dancer choose one male patron to sit in a chair on stage and be a part of the performance; we usually choose the youngest guy in the club as a sort of "handing down the torch" to the next generation of men to carry on this oldest of business's (for my last dance I am going to choose that sweetheart of a college kid- he needs it). It's actually quite weird in a way, however still beautiful all at the same time. I get it though now, I understand from all the years I have been here what this job, this fantasy is all about.

Most male patrons say they come because they want a place to not worry about being politically correct or well behaved. They just want to relax, get aroused, and be a man. Our culture encourages the creation of Man Spaces, because the straight male sex drive is "normal," and anything else is considered deviant. If you step into a strip club, you essentially are stepping into the male libido in its ultimate and natural form. This club strips away society's ability to cover up the raw truth of man and woman and its constant quest to cover it with window dressing. There is no such thing as "civilization," only the illusion we are given and that we all go along with to make ourselves feel better about our natural impulses.

Anyways, I have made my way back stage now to get ready for my final dance. The rest of the girls are helping me look my best; my eye-liner is dark with a hint of blue streak along with my body being covered in the Maui Babe to give my skin that glossy smooth texture. My outfit tonight consists of a black Satin bra from Allure with pink trim and incrusted diamonds around the outer lining, along with a high thread count black laced thong garnished with a tastefully Satin black garter belt from Leg Avenue. I have practiced for this dance and have been so for a week now. I have incorporated a lot of my usual moves for the lap dance portion of the dance along with some of Lady Gaga's choreography from her "Bad Romance" music video (not the creepy thriller moves though-just the sexier body movements during the chorus of that song).

The song "Gypsy" is a good choice for the leaving dancers I think: It is a dialogue between a guy and a girl. And the guy's thinking of leaving and exploring the world on his own. We have those moments; the sweet taste of freedom. But he has her. And she has him. And he's thinking of leaving her so that he can "see the whole world in front of him." Devastated, she could only come up with saying something that can maybe help her cope from the pain. Saying the words "I don't want to be alone forever, but I can be tonight" - Imagine the strength. You got slapped in the face, and your only reaction is "I'll be alright. I mean, I won't be forever, but I'll manage tonight."

The guy then asks her "Why do we love each other?"

And she could only reply "Honey, it's simple: it's the way that you love and treat your mother."

The guy in the song then learns that he doesn't need to see the world alone. He doesn't need to wander of the Earth's wonders. He doesn't have to be alone.

He has her. And she has him.

And finally he thinks of not staying with her but letting her come with him. "Thought that I would be alone forever, but I won't be tonight. I'm a man without a home, but I think with you, I could spend my life."

We're all waiting for that person to say those words to us.

We're all gypsies in a way. I am no different from you or anyone.

See the world together. Never alone.

This is it. The music has started, and the curtain has opened. Smoke fills the stage and the lights struggle to peak through like the sun's rays during overcast. I am your private dancer for one last time. I no longer dance for money, and any song will just not do. I dance for my freedom, and this is that perfect song. You will never see "Diamond" ever again, for this is my last show and illusion. I am now a Gypsy and wanderer like everyone else out there in the world, looking for something more than just a parlor trick.

FLIGHT DISCRETION

Newark, New Jersey 2006

FREEDOM AIR FL 117 contact Newark Tower on
118.300 for final approach is squawked over the
COMM1 as this turnaround flight from Fort
Lauderdale starts to come to an end. It's been a long
day for me and hearing those words for instructions
of final approach, into anywhere for that matter,
always washes over me with a sense of relief and
calm. Those guys and gals on the ground in those
towers are my only friends in the sky (besides my
crew) who guide me and are my extra eyes and ears.
It has always amazed me how this machine, this
highway in the sky functions, everyday 24/7 with
limited disasters and serious errors because if you
think about it, it all hangs by a very small thread. It

may seem peaceful to you as a passenger, but it is actually organized chaos in the background.

I've been flying for 11 years now, and there is not a day that passes where I see something that is astonishing. The images I see from the cockpit are always worthy of a Kodak moment or calendar spread. My favorites are autumn sunsets over the North Eastern sea board, or just sunsets in general. On the ground or up 10 or 20,000 feet is a sight that few are fortunate to see. The electric yellows, reds, and oranges for some reason are magnified to the point where I question if reality up here is in some form of new HD than down below. There is a tremendous sense freedom when I am up here, however, there are so many rules and regulations that cast a shadow over that feeling, a lot of them for good reason, and some that are rather stupid if you'd ask me.

Some FAA rules are just fucking brainless. Like the fact that when we're at 39,000 feet going 400 miles an hour, in a plane that could hit turbulence at any minute, (flight attendants) can walk around and serve hot coffee and Chateaubriand. But when we're on the ground, on a flat piece of asphalt going five to ten miles an hour, they've got to be buckled in like they're a driver in the Michigan 500. The one rule I do happen to agree with though is the one about cell phones. What can happen on a plane if you so choose to use those glowing oracles you have in your hand when asked not too? Well, what can happen is if 12 people decide to call someone just before landing, I can get a false reading on my instruments saying that we are higher than we really are. If that happens is there a possibility of me plunging the plane into the ground like a suicidal lunatic? Yes. The newspapers would have a field day for the next few months posturing rumors of a drunken pilot with a troubled past for someone to blame until the black box is recovered; and full autopsy of the plane and its instrument readings would reveal the real truth that cell phones do in fact kill people, literally.

We don't make you stow your laptop because we're worried about electronic interference. It's about having a projectile on your lap. I don't know about you, but I don't want to get hit in the head by a MacBook going 200 miles per hour. And we're not trying to ruin your fun by making you take off your headphones. We just want you to be able to hear us if there's an emergency; oh yeah and by the way, there is no such thing as a "water landing," it's called crashing into the fucking ocean. Also, the Department of Transportation has put such an emphasis on on-time performance that we pretty much aren't allowed to delay a flight anymore, even if there are 20 people on a connecting flight that's coming in just a little late. No, it's not your imagination: Airlines really have adjusted their flight arrival times so they can have a better record of on-time arrivals. So they might say a flight takes two hours when it really takes an hour and 45 minutes.

Speaking of on-time, our flight right now is, and I have just informed one of our new flight attendants (I think her name is Shelby) that we are about to make our final into New Jersey. Man, am I glad to hear her voice over the intercom, that woman is something else I tell ya. She just joined our flight crew rotation about a month ago and she is a firecracker. I always see all the guys in the airport lounges hoover around her like a pack of German U-boats waiting to sink their torpedoes into her haul.

Who could blame them? She looks like Scarlett Johansson when she starred in that movie The Island; when she was in her prime. I am a big sucker for the blondes though. I try not to make a big fuss over her, but Christ on an fucking cracker do I ever get my tongue twisted when I am around her or even speak to her over the intercom about the simplest things.

She is a mystery; we (the male pilots) are still trying to figure out her seniority and age since all the female attendants mess with us by changing the hems on their skirts. It's a clever little trick they do to mess with us I must say. Shelby has this glint of an attitude about her though beneath her pleasant and friendly customer service. It's what separates her from the rest in my view. You can see it in her hazel eyes; eye's that look like the Irish countryside after a morning rain. It's in her walk, the way she flirts with her butt, and the way she moves her hips in a slight rotation.

Normally I don't have a problem picking up women with this job status, however, Shelby makes you feel like you're that 8 year old boy who wants that brand new hot toy for Christmas, not knowing if

Santa will hear your calls of gimme, gimme, gimme! Anyways, I should probably focus on flying this plane anyways. I guess this is why they call it the "cockpit" since this is where my cock belongs right now. I am responsible for 180 souls today, so I should save the day-dreaming and spank-bank fantasies for later. Whatever, though. There will always be more Shelby's- beauty is common in this world.

I am glad we are on final right now (I am so tired), I now have visual on the airport and I am about to turn our heading in order to parallel the airport to set us up for the final approach; we are currently number two for landing behind a regional carrier. Our work rules allow us to be on duty 16 hours without a break. That's many more hours than a truck driver. And unlike a truck driver, who can pull over at the next rest stop, we can't pull over at the next cloud. Do pilots sleep in (the cockpit)? Have I slept in here? Definitely. Sometimes it's just a ten-minute catnap, but it happens.

When you get on that airplane at 7 a.m., you want your pilot to be rested and ready. But the hotels they put us in now are so bad that there are many nights when I toss and turn. They're in bad neighborhoods, they're loud, they've got bedbugs, and there have been stabbings in the parking lot. Sometimes the airline won't give us lunch breaks or even time to eat. We have to delay flights just so we can get food. I am actually dying right now for an airport burger. They are fucking expensive and not worth the coin, but I don't care at this point.

People always ask, "What's the scariest thing that's ever happened to you?" I tell them it was a van ride from the Los Angeles airport to the hotel, and I'm not kidding. Up here with me, you are as safe as you can be. Your chances of dying today with me are slim, so slim I am not even going to recite some stupid statistic because it is not even worth the effort. Also, it's true also that landing is probably one of the most challenging things we do up here. So if you want to say something nice to a pilot as you're getting off the plane, say 'Nice landing.' We do appreciate that.

Speaking of landings, we have just been cleared by Newark Tower to land on Runway 22R. Conditions are looking good, except for a slight crosswind that I will have to adjust to with my rudder and yawing skills. I can see the runway now. It always looks so beautiful this time of night. The light's guide me home to its threshold. It is a strip of whites, reds and greens to which show me the path to the end of a good day. There is no better feeling in the world than seeing the VASI/PAPI lights and slope indicator telling me that I am on target.

White over white you're high as a kite / you'll fly all night.
Red over white you're all right.
Red over red you're dead.

Hitting the threshold at the center of the runway is like hitting a home run, or scoring with the hot chick when you were in high school. It is the ultimate high. This is what I live for.

I am your Sheppard in the sky. I will take you to your grandparent's house for Christmas and Thanksgiving holidays, your trip to Mali, or your Spring Break to Cancun. I will take you to where ever you desire to go in this world. I will be a part of your final arrival.

A MIDNIGHT STROLL WITH A VEGAS VAGABOND

Las Vegas, Nevada 1989

THIS IS THE LAND OF OPPORTUNITY, GET LOST! - Is screamed out a passenger window at some poor Latino man, and probably an illegal that just rolled in off the rails from crossing our lightly defended border to the south. "Get lost," huh- what did that fucking piece of shit asshole even mean? We are all lost, aren't we? This whole country is lost. I am lost, like a red-headed step-child born from the seed of an eager yardman, and the compliance of loose legs.

I have to live with empty eyes as I stumble cross this boulevard day in and day out. This town spreads evil thick and pan at every turn, every corner, and in every room. There are broken promises and broken pride all around me and it keeps me down and along for the ride.

I look for the grace of God in stranger's arms and hands everyday just to get by; only to be spent and sent back into the black hole that is this city: a giant casino. I have a problem. I want so desperately to leave this place, but this city holds me hostage at every chance. It's a drug I can't shake, a high I have to chase. I am in an abusive relationship with her; Lady Luck that is. She is my salvation, yet will be my ultimate demise. She gives me what I need when I can afford her, only to leave me by the curb; broke, bruised, and with the dry taste of warm Vodka in my mouth. I give her that pedestal to stand on over me because she has a hold on my attention, a control I can never break from. A heart I could never club. A kiss I can never fold. She blinded me with her twins of happiness.

The neon lights offer a sense of comfort at night, this is home. Like a moth to a lamp, I can't resist. I am just like any other fucking asshole that comes here with his wallet opened, begging for a chance to hit it big and escape this giant gutter-ball. Escape the *humdrum of the suburbs, the HR halfwits, the slums, the hoops, and the fucking human race. Home is a desperate end though. I am just trying to pick my feelings undone. Las Vegas is the ultimate carnival town, and I am a sucker- just like the rest of the jagoffs who claim to bleed the Red, White, and Blue. The only color they will be bleeding here is Green. The friends they lose here will be up to them as well. Will it be all their Benjamin's? Their Jackson's and Grant's, or will they just lose some Washington's in a sea of panties, perfume, and lap dances? What about their real friends back home- their wives, husbands, children and families? I know of that kind of loss too; a loss that can never be filled by any win, thrill, trick, fuck, snort, or illusion.*

I used to have it decent -a white stucco house in a college town. No real problems I needed to drown back in those days, just a few. I used to go to class just to pass the time with no real direction. Where I was going I didn't really mind because I had all I ever wanted. I was always born lost come to think of it though; always a drifter in my mind and spirit. Not having a father around didn't help for sure. Well he was never at home always up in his "tower" working on whatever White-Collars do. I had no real direction and any male role models that I can think of, they all consisted of my loser uncles and my mom's many neanderthalic lovers.

I used to have an old acoustic that showed me how to score. Not anymore now though. I lost it as collateral at one of the tables at The Venetian. The best I can do now is call up some of Vegas' lower totem pole call-girl's for maybe 10 minutes if the tourists are nice to me today. I used to know of a girl back in Boca Raton, Florida (where I used to live) who always taught me about what I couldn't have. Maybe she always knew deep down of what I would eventually become; a lonely drifter whose Jansen Sport, and $50 to his name, being the only unchanging personal legacy to offer.

It seems like yesterday that Isabella gave me that look of utter annoyance when I asked her out to Chili's after one of our marketing lectures. I wonder what I would hear about her if I called that girl now to see where she is and how great her life must be. Who am I kidding though? She is probably married, with two kids and a rich husband for all I know. She *was always an intelligent girl that Isabella. Plus, I can't even afford to call her let alone muster up enough courage to even speak. I am a little drunk and high as shit.*

*This is the price I have paid for calling on what I thought was my destiny. The river had to run wild just that one night. I thought I could beat the odds and take this town for everything it had. I was **somebody** here at one point, a long time ago. A time when cocaine was the new hip thing and when everyone was afraid of AIDS. A time when guitar, synth and Sax solo's filled a songs bridge and artists made music because it made people happy. Now those same artists are here. They have come back here to die in a way.*

Las Vegas is God's waiting room for old performers and musicians; waiting before that last curtain call and applause for being part of someone's night, anniversary, bachelor party, Shot-gun Wedding and girl's weekend. People once knew me, women knew me. The spotlights used to shine for me at night, and only for me. I can still taste the neon-glitter in my mouth from the countless desperate hussies who wanted a shot with me. I smell of that same desperation now; the smell of cheap cigarettes and last night's discarded Rye.

Now those same lights mock me at every turn as I walk past the places I used to take her- the sweetheart I once had here in this town. The house she used to live in before she made it big. I walk down the streets she once did, the streets that are still in her blood; her roots. Her music was high and sweet I tell ya, then she just blew away like a paper bag caught in an updraft. Now instead of people offering me things, I stand here for theirs. I beg for forgiveness through my glare, but no one hears my cries. Why should they? It's my own fault. I am a product of my culture and generation. I had no control. I ran with the devil, so I have no one else to blame.

All I ever wanted was a taste, and I had it. It's understood that I had to reach for it and let the wheels of fortune spin. My only mistake though was touching his fiery hand and allowing the clouds to come crashing in. It wasn't good enough though, she wasn't good enough. It sits like a dagger in my back now. I put it there myself. The best thing I can look forward to these days is the shade of a palm tree during the blistering days out here. I am lost, that's for sure. I fell from grace and now I can't escape the prison to which I lost everything too. The patrons to this city, the ones I despise and used to love are the only ones who keep me alive now. It's one of life's hilarious ironies.

Some days I wander this town in hopes of actually getting lost for good. In the vein wish that I may escape this all if I just walk aimlessly in one direction. I can't though. A part of me wants it all back, the way it was when she was on my side. If given the chance I won't fold on her kiss like I did. I will look at my destiny instead of her twins of happiness. I'll trump her Heart with Diamonds; a lady's best friend. It wasn't supposed to be this way. The odds were so slim and near impossible, yet I still lost in the end; that wild river screwed me and washed away my identity, my sins.

This is the land of opportunity after all. I have nothing left to lose.

My dream isn't over yet. It's not time for me to wake up.

This dust land fairy tale of mine has no end.

FRUSTRATIONS OF A FLIGHT ATTENDANT

Fort Lauderdale, Florida 2006

WE EXPECT MILD TURBULANCE, announces our Captain on this in-bound flight from Chicago's O'Hare. Sure enough, like clock-work I can see most, if not all, of the passengers passing anxious glances at each other as if the words "Mild" and "Turbulence" put together were the worst thing they have heard in their entire lives. More than two million people fly in the United States each day and yet since 1980 only three people have died as a direct result of turbulence.

Of those fatalities, two passengers weren't wearing their safety belts. During that same time period, the Federal Aviation Administration recorded just over 300 serious injuries from turbulence, and more than two-thirds of the victims were flight attendants. What do these numbers mean? As long as your seat belt is on, you're more likely to be injured by falling luggage than by choppy air. So when I see people rolling their eyes about the threat of turbulence, I hope they realize that if anyone is going to get to ride home in an ambulance/garner an emergency landing, it will be for me.

I like my job and all, but holy shit, do I ever *hate* getting put on these flights into places like West Palm Beach, Lauderdale or Vail; the passengers all think they're in first class, even though that's impossible. They don't do what we ask, and all the overhead bins are full of fucking mink coats and Louis Vuitton bags that can fit a bowling ball or small dog in. Whatever, I am not even surprised anymore, and I actually get a good laugh out if it anyways.

It's a thankless job half the time; I mean really, I don't get paid much for even a quarter of the things I have to put up with on a daily basis. Would it kill anyone to say a simple "Hello there Shelby" or smile when they step in? We are after all about to fly across the sky and be crammed in a giant tube at 23,000 feet for a few hours; it's a very intimate experience if you think about it. Also, you know all that pre-flight time when we're cramming bags into overhead bins? None of that shows up in our paychecks. Flight attendants get paid for "flight hours only." Translation: The clock doesn't start until the pilot contacts Ground Control and we push away from the gate. Flight delays, cancellations, and layovers affect us just as much as they do passengers—maybe even more. Airlines aren't completely heartless, though. From the time we sign in at the airport until the plane slides back into the gate at our home base, we get an expense allowance of $1.50 an hour. It's not much, but it helps.

Seriously though, does anyone even pay attention to me when I am up here at the front giving the safety tips and pre-flight instructions? The guys are for sure, but to what reason I am still not quite sure. Given by the glazed glances the gentleman in seat D13B is giving me right now, I think it's safe to say that he is not really interested in my pointing skills or my ability to show him how to secure the oxygen mask to the face in case his vacation turns into a living nightmare.

I am a 26, blonde, and thinly toned woman. So my guess is he has noticed the way in which these stupid heels the airline makes us wear creates the illusion that my butt is more lifted and toned than it already is along with my thigh and calve muscles. Heels are a double edged sword for women; they are murder on the feet, yet are friends to our figure. I would be lying though if I said I didn't like the attention I get doing this job. All women like attention; it makes us feel good, wanted and sexy.

I don't get to wear the short skirts yet though which kind of sucks in a way. Oh yeah, I forgot to mention that about the hierarchy and seniority on this job. Our tenure doesn't just determine which routes we fly and which days we get to take off, but it also affects the hierarchy in our crash pad, an apartment shared by as many as 20 flight attendants. Seniority is the difference between top or lower bunk, what floor your bed is on, and just how far away your room is from noisy areas such as doors or stairwells. Seniority even determines the length of our skirts— we can't hem them above a certain length until we're off probation.

Afterward, it's OK to shorten the hem and show a little leg. Some of the friskier pilots take advantage of the long hems; they know that new hires tend to be more flattered by their advances than senior flight attendants. One senior flight attendant I know intentionally left her skirt long just to trick keep these pilots interested even though she was older and had seniority! That bitch. Whatever, competition is everywhere in the world of women, and I take it as a compliment since I am younger, tighter, and hotter. No matter the hem, I'll still win.

Speaking of competition, it is fierce for this job. When our airline announced 1,000 openings a few years back when I applied, it received over 100,000 applications. Even Harvard's acceptance rate isn't that low! All that competition means that most applicants who score interviews have college degrees—I know doctors and lawyers who've made the career switch. But you don't need a law degree to get your foot in the jet-way door. The 4 percent who do get a callback interview really need to weigh the pros and cons of the job. As we like to say, flight attendants must be willing to cut their hair and go anywhere.

And if you can't survive on $18,000 a year, most new hires' salary, don't even think about applying honey.

The best though is seeing the covert competition between me and the wives/girlfriends of the male passengers on board today. The age old battle began as soon as they all stepped off the jet-way and into my domain. Take for instance the woman sitting in seat D15A right now in front of me. She has been giving me the bitch stare the moment her husband asked for the cart menu.

I get it though- I am an instinctual threat to her life, her world, and marriage. I know you can take care of your husband honey (is what I want to say to her) but I will be the one taking care of him today; this is my plane after all and the guy looks like he could use a good fantasy. She isn't ugly or anything, she is actually quite cute in a Pam off of *The Office* sort of way. However, she and I have both noticed her husband checking me out as if he were an art connoisseur (you think by now at his age he would know how to be discreet) and I don't blame him. He is a man, and it's in man's nature to look, and want more. It's a biological instinct that date back to the beginning of time. Without it, there would be no perpetuation of the species and diversification of the gene pool.

I am sure he loves his wife and all, but comparing me to her would be like comparing Gucci to Macy's clothing- Macy's will give you what you *need* at a reasonable price, and Gucci will give you what you *want* at an expensive cost. This dude should stop starring at me now, or I will cost him a lecture from his wife later tonight (and maybe even his marriage on down the road if he keeps ignoring her for woman like me- whom is *way* out of his league). This guy needs to drive a Ford Focus. I'm a Ferrari he wouldn't know how to handle.

That's the problem I have though: getting attention from every, and all men, when all I really want is for just the hot, confident, un-married and good-looking ones to gawk at me. Yet it seems like it's just all the guys who look like John Turturro from the film Big Lebowski or the business men who look like John Goodman or Steve Buscemi who stare at my goods and ask pointless questions about which brand of cookies the airline uses just get a closer view of my cash and prizes. I have even had a guy flat-out ask me what I was doing later, and if I wanted to join him at a party in Dallas this one time last year. Sorry buddy, you have been watching too many movies. I don't have time to play your little game of fish since I usually have a quick red-eye after the day flight or an early domestic gig in the morning.

While we are on the topic of sex, it amazes me how people think I don't notice when they are trying to join the 'Mile High Club.' It's usually on the long flights overseas when the line of people waiting to use the bathroom gives them away, and nine times out of ten, it's a passenger who asks the flight attendants to intervene. Strictly speaking, it's not against the law to join the 'Mile High Club,' but it is against the law to disobey crew member commands. If I ask you to stop doing whatever it is you're doing, by all means, stop! Otherwise, you're going to have a very awkward conversation when you meet your cell mate. How do people mange to do it or accomplish anything worthy in there anyways? You would have to be a member of cirque du soleil to get your partner into a take-off position.

That's the other thing though that pisses me off a lot of the time; that people think us female Flight Attendants have a man in every city that we blow off steam with after our one-ways and connecting flights. Our median age is 44, most of us are either married, have one partner, or like me, just don't really care right now since I am young and so busy all the time; again people watch too many movies these days or don't take them for what most of them are- fiction mixed with a bit of truth and hyperbole.

I would be lying though if I had never thought about the idea, or taking a good-looking guy on the plane back to the hotel room. It gets lonely sometimes doing this kind of job even though I am constantly surrounded by people. The last action I had was with one of my male co-workers, which was fun, but will probably be a huge and awkward mistake once we see each other again; we aren't always with the same team of pilots and attendants, depending on scheduling.

My real pet peeve though besides what I was just saying, is Diet Coke. No, I am not a Pepsi girl or a promoter of the company (although it would be nice to get paid to do so on the side) it's just because Diet Coke, for whatever reason, takes the most time to pour-the fizz takes forever to settle at 35,000 feet. In the time it takes me to pour a single cup of Diet Coke, I can serve three passengers a different beverage. So even though giving cans to first-class passengers is a big no-no, you'll occasionally spy 12 ounces of silver trimmed in red sitting up there.

Anyways, the people aren't so bad. I can tolerate all the rudeness, comments, and whining because in a way I understand all of it. Our lives for the most part suck. We in this country work long hours, get paid shit, and don't get laid much. That's half a lie, sorry. What I meant to say is that people get screwed everyday in this country, but by their government; a system to which we all have to run around in because we have nowhere else to hide anymore and enjoy life and its true meaning. So when people get time off of the rat-race to go on a vacation they demand to be treated like first-class, and they deserve it. The mink coats in the overhead are starting to make sense now. I am glad to be a part of that vacation for sure. The only frustration and question I have left for myself though is how can I avoid that race I don't care to run? I would rather be like that Diet Coke that keeps on fizzing, that never becomes flat. In a way, with this job I am always going on vacation: L.A, Frankfurt, London-Heathrow, Hong Kong, Vancouver, Cape Town, Fiji, Sydney, Miami, Florence, and Dubai. I am on vacation 24/7, 365.

CONFESSIONS OF A
WALL STREET INSIDER

10:08 am Monday October 8th, 2025
To: Rachel Lennox (r.lennox@iberry.com)
From: John Fantelli (fantellij@iberry.com)

Rachel,

Of all the times I could have written you back, I write you now in my darkest of days, a calm before the storm if you will. I don't even know if this is still your imail account, I don't really know if this will even reach you, but I would hate myself even more if I had never tried.

Look, I know you despise my guts and soul; I would too from all the shit I put you through, us through. In fact I hate myself now more than ever before because I am a part of this fucking mess and it's something I can never, will never, live down. However, you need to heed this message and hear me out.

Please, just this once.

Right now, as I stare at the big board I am taken aback as it is a sea of green: S&P +50, DJI +280, TSX +250, NASDAQ + 40. Europe as well is about to finish the day brighter than the greenest of Christmas trees (remember those when we were young?); it will all be red by next week. The media is playing the spin game well again, distracting the hopeless gullible people of this country away from the fact that the administration is in panic mode as I type this.

That whole story you probably heard about in the NY Post regarding FEMA along with Homeland Security, NORAD, and other agencies doing "domestic terror" drills all month is as much of a lie as what this country has become; one giant farce. There aren't going to be any drills, the "drills" will be for real this time. It's just a cover for mobilization and the continuity of government that's about to unfold.

There are reports that the department of Homeland Security is engaged in a massive, covert military build-up. An article in the associated press in February confirmed another open purchase order by DHS for 1.6 billion rounds of ammunition. According to an op-ed in Forbes, that's enough to sustain an Iraq-sized war for over twenty years. DHS has also acquired heavily armoured tanks, which have been seen roaming the streets. Evidently somebody in government is expecting some serious civil unrest. They have been getting prepared for the big crash that will happen this week sometime after the markets close on Thursday. You will start to see some big news come out of China about our debt situation.

The Chinese have wanted to recall their U.S treasury holdings ever since 2013 when we raised the nation's debt ceiling yet again. Basically, what I am trying to say is the carnival of fake money is over Rachel. The game is up. You need to get out of your city now; they will become death-traps when this all happens: New York, Los Angeles, Chicago, and Miami, all of them. If you still work at that hotel back in our home town just leave, call in sick the next day, whatever you have to do.

What will happen soon is the direct result of protocols that were set up long ago:

When Thursday comes, when the U.S. treasury declares a force majeure on debt, it will not be broad-casted on mainstream media. There's no sense because the American people won't even understand what it means- but the announcement would actually be put on the federal reserve wire system, which would, of course, immediately be picked up by all media outlets anyway. The U.S. treasury would declare a force majeure on debt after the Asian and European markets closed, probably at 12:30 p.m. EDT. The reason why that hour was always selected is because Asian and European markets close. It's also the lunch hour for the markets. It's when you're going to have the fewest people on the floor of the exchanges. That will be the ideal time to make such an announcement.

A few seconds after that announcement is made all United States markets, both equities debt and commodities (i.e., stock, bonds, commodities, which have trading collars or permissible daily limits) would all be limit-offered with pools. Limit-offered means that there are more sellers at the limit (i.e., limit down, than there are buyers).

So-called 'pools' would immediately begin to form, probably a thousand contracts every few minutes. 'limit-offered with pools' - this is trader language i know but hear me out. Pools to sell 2,000 lots, 3,000 lots. That means, the number of sellers over and above the available buyers at the limit-offered price. That will begin to build.

By 1:00 P.M, the news will begin to sink in because it would take awhile before panic selling would arise from the public. This news is going to be released at lunch hour. A lot of the American people initially would not even understand the temerity of the news. You will see professional selling first, and as that professional selling intensified over the afternoon, the sec, the CFTC, NASDAQ, and various market regulatory authorities would begin to institute certain emergency market protocols. This would be the installation of the so-called 'declaration of fast market conditions, for instance; the declaration of 'no more stop orders,' the declaration of 'fill at any price,' etc. in a desperate bid to maintain liquidity.

That first day, the Dow Jones industrial average and related indices on a percentage basis will lose about 20% of their value by the close of business that day. The real impact will come overnight when the American people find out what this was all about and when it is explained to them.

At 7:30 a.m. EDT, the Tokyo markets will open, and no price would be affixed for probably three or four hours into the session due to the avalanche of selling. Once prices are established, the government of Japan will close all of its financial markets. European markets will not even open. All European governments will close all capital exchanges the next day.

The United States will, in order to accommodate global electronic trading, attempt to open the market on the second day, which they will do, regardless of price, just to maintain some liquidity. At the end of day two, the Dow Jones and related indices, will have lost around two thirds of their value, and prices will be set accordingly.

On day three, the New York stock exchange, the sec and other related agencies will recommend to the United States treasury and the Federal Reserve that all markets be closed. That will be on the morning of day three. At 11:00 a.m., the Federal Reserve will then order all domestic banks closed. All of the twelve Federal Reserve district banks will (30 minutes later) have special U.S. forces parachuted in and around them to secure whatever gold bullion reserves they had left.

Day three, 9:00 p.m. (and this is especially import Rachel), the President of the United States will declare a state of martial law. All financial transactions will come to an end. The treasury would act to formally de-monetize the U.S. dollar and declare it worthless. This will be totally unprecedented. In the past, collapses have been temporary and have been brought back up. But what I am talking about now, and have been privy to, is the end.

These protocols that I'm referring to aren't even all that secret. They were publicly available all through the Clinton era. These are treasury protocols that were instituted mostly in the late 1970s when the treasury and Federal Reserve began to feel that it was important to have an emergency-collapse protocol in place. I hope by now you understand how serious this all is and what it all means.

Look out your window Rachel. Tell me what you see. You see the same things that you see every day. Well, imagine you've never seen it. Imagine you spent your whole life in other parts of the world, being told everyday that this {America} is the land of the free. You start to want to get some of that "freedom" for yourself. Then you finally decide you've had enough and you finally get here and realize that it's all a lie, that it's not all rainbows and orgasms over here. Look at the people around you. You tell me which ones are truly free. Free from debt. Anxiety. Stress. Fear. Failure. Shame. Infidelity.

How many of those people I see down below wish that they were born knowing what they know now or even by this time next week? Are we really that better off than our enemies, the ones who we think are the terrorists and despots? Ask yourself how many would do things the same way over again, and how many would live their lives like me.

I am nothing but a prisoner in my own personal hell that I helped create without even knowing, everyone did the same. compliance and compartmentalization, that's all it really takes, and the worst part about it all is that it was so obvious if we just stopped everything for just one moment in time and looked around and up for once.

For Christ sake Rachel, how could we have been so stupid and irresponsible! How could I have been so gullible? They say history repeats itself, it's not true. History echoes at us and we see events that have happened before take place again and again just in a different context. We never learn because we are all too arrogant! We forget that we are not gods here on earth at that one day eventually our hubris and ignorance would come back to haunt us.

I'm looking out my window right now, and today see something much different than what will be seen very soon. It's like I am looking at one of those old black and white photos from a museum that will be found in the future. I see people calmly milling about on the corner of Wall and Hanover Street sipping on $20.00 lattes in front of the homeless tents. I see a police car with its light-bar on- probably responding to another Thought Crime or protestor of our new Death Care law executed by our dear leader and chief. I see a man at his desk across the street wearing ear phones and starring at his i-screen.

I imagine him listening to that old song "New York Minute" by Don Henley as he works away on soon to be meaningless hedge fund data reports. I envision him going home to his wife tonight, even his kids perhaps. He will get to kiss her, hold her, smell her perfume and maybe even make love to her like he normally would. I wish I could tell him to cherish the night, treasure his wife and kids, and that I hope he has done so since the day they met for tomorrow and forever after, it will be anything but normal for his family. That is the only guarantee I give him.

By now you are probably wondering why you. Why are you the first and last person I will tell this to? I can't give you a simple answer to that, it's frankly because even if you did tell someone, no one would believe you. Or, maybe it's the gifted Jim Beam speaking that I found in my office drawer. Maybe it's because the young women I saw behind the Starbucks counter this morning reminded me of you in the past. Or maybe it's the selfish truth that you represent a time when I knew who I was, and that in hopes of saving you I will be saving a part of myself, my true self. Those two people are two entities I know I can never fully get back. It's too late. I screwed up with you, with us, and now with this country.

Don't ever think that I didn't love you. I'll always remember you: that girl with the ocean blues that did a double-take of me in the lobby of that lecture hall, the one who I then by coincidence met for a second time physically at that Halloween party a week later, the girl who tried to open her heart to me while we watched the rangers beat the leafs, the girl who believed in the real me for the longest time, but was soon unknowingly fooled by my shadow.

You will in no doubt see me on the news very soon; things will be said about me; awful things, most of them true, and many that will be false as to cover up the very facts that will be revealed eventually through this countries now destined and unstoppable course. If you don't believe me right now you soon will later this week. It doesn't matter who you reveal this information or warning to because it's not relevant anymore. Panic will ensue either way. The truth of our situation will be unbearable for this country, and its people. The illusion will be broken. I won't be sticking around this place, this city, or world long enough now to deal with it anyway. I am tired, tired of it all, all the lies, keeping them straight. It's exhausting.

As a final wish, I would like you to remember me not as the man you have likely grown to hate, or the man you will see on the front page this week, but as that guy you once took a second look at back in the entrance of that lecture hall. The guy I too once believed in.

CALL-GIRL CONFESSIONAL

Miami, Florida 1995

HIDDEN SECRETS: SENATOR TAKING PUBLIC SERVICE TO NEW LEVELS is printed on the front page of a Wall Street Journal that has floated by my feet as I wait for my town car. From what I have heard through the media, a Senator from our district has been caught using tax-payer money to run his own underground brothel here in Florida- a secret that has been kept well hidden for some time.

Secrets, I have many. We all do. This city has many, and deep dark ones which you will only find behind rich oak doors that contain wealthy old white men drinking Whiskey in smoke-filled merriment. Hell, half the skyscrapers here in Miami were built on cocaine money from the drug-running days of the 80's. Well those days are far behind me now. It was in 1986 when I first started college only to drop out two years later after finding out that I could make more money doing this than I ever would working as some office bitch or in some managerial position.

It wasn't a sudden realization though. It all started out slow; a tip toeing journey into realization. I began stripping out at this place called Bare Necessities off of South Dixie Highway near the Dadeland rail station. I had no choice. I was down on my rent, and my parents could have given two shits about me and my schooling. It was a good enough gig though, and I had the body and looks for it too.

I was 19, thin with that hour-glass curve that made all the guys salivate like starved retrievers waiting for their kibble. I cleared an average $500 a night depending on if I was to entertain a high roller in the "Closet." We called the back-room that because the girls and I always joked about how it reminded us of the days in High School where at parties we used to play that game called "Would You Rather" in the host's basement. It's funny now looking back how similar the activities that took place in both "closets" were. Things never change I guess, just the context of them.

Like most girls my age, I thought I would get in, make my green, and get out before I became too jaded and my soul sucked dry. That wasn't the case though, the money was too good, and the stuff you learn on the street, the truth, for me far outweighed anything I would learn from a book. After working at Bare Necessities, I managed through contacts to score a gig with one of the most highly used escort services in all of Florida. It was starting there when I truly began to see how fucked up our world is and why everything has to be so secret in mine.

I was always an intelligent girl. I got mostly straight "A's" throughout middle school and in my first two years of college I still managed to impress my professors. So you must be thinking to yourself by now, "Isabella, you're an intelligent girl, why live the life your living when you could just be normal?" Well, I would say to that, what do you mean by normal? And how is this "normal" life you speak of any different from what I am doing? I would actually debate with you and argue that what I do is actually more "normal" and "intelligent" than anything else society infers to you.

I represent the honest truth, reality in its rawest form. I represent one of life's dirty little secrets. I provide a service to which is always in demand and will never run dry. The demand in my field far outweighs the quality of supply (we are talking about pussy of course) If you're a business major, isn't that called a lucrative market? And isn't it intelligent to exploit that market for personal gain? I think so. We, after all, do live in the land of Capitalism. What is more capitalistic, better yet, what is more *American* than what I do?

Its people's distinctions between call-girls and the ordinary are what piss me off the most. They presume that call-girls or prostitutes are fundamentally different from what we in the biz call "Green Bush," "Amateurs," or "Gold Diggers" if you like, which we are neither. Peoples assumptions seems to be based on the fallacies that a) prostitutes provide a consistent level of service no matter how we are treated; and b) to a man, all sex and any sex is good. While the second statement may be certainly true for some of the men I've been with and men in general (especially those who patronize streetwalkers) it isn't by any stretch of the imagination true of most.

The average client of a $300/hour call-girl (which is exactly what I charge) wants a good, quality what we in the biz call a "Girlfriend Experience" (GFE), which will be much more likely if he treats his "date" like a lady (i.e. holds the door open for her, brings flowers etc). Most escorts who are treated as though they are "bought and paid for" will try to complete the experience as quickly as possible and get such a client out the door.

My experience is that the typical client enjoys the illusion that a beautiful woman wants to spend time with him, even if he intellectually knows she is there and using him for his money (you may equate this to "Gold Diggers" in the "normal" world) However, with me and girls of my kind we offer the client a sure thing, even though we are getting paid. In the "normal" world there is sometimes no guarantee of needs being met. I guarantee you that the majority of my clients tried their utmost to impress me, even to the point of bringing me gifts, flowers, and the like which I always found weird since that is what you do in the "normal" world of non-vice. You may be also wondering-like I have been for quite some time- as to why they do this.

Well, the clearest answer that I can give to you, and to myself, is that Prostitution is evolutionarily familiar because mating is evolutionarily familiar and prostitutes (at least the classy ones) are no different from "normal" Gold-Diggers whom men also have to pay – not in cash payments but in dinners and movies, gifts, flowers, chocolates, and motor oil – if they wanted to impress them enough to have sex with them. I see this all over Miami and the country alike. I used to hear it from my old girlfriends (before they disowned me because of what I "do") that they would not sleep with a man until he proved that he "loved" them by buying her shiny trinkets, dinners, and drinks at the bar. How delusional is that? My clients are intelligent. I am intelligent.

The intelligent man knows that free tail is always the most expensive; resources of time and money. Intelligent men are less likely to believe the propaganda against women like myself, and less likely to have the kind of brittle masculine ego which would be wounded by "having to pay for it," and can make a pragmatic decision to spend their hard earned money on a "sure thing" rather than chasing women whose price and quality uncertain.

So who are the real losers? This world to me is upside down. It's all so delusional to the point where people seem to do anything and everything to suppress their guilt about what they want and need in life. We women in both the legal world and the world of vice win either way. It's only the men in my world who get "theirs" at the same time I get "mine." It's a shame really. Plus I like sex. Most women do, if not more than men.

What now you say? I am crazy for even implying such a fallacy? In case you have been living under a rock for all of time, we have something on our body that exists for the sole purpose of sexual pleasure. That's another one of life's dirty little secrets honey. Yet it's suppressed at every turn in our society. It's like there is a secret war going on between women in our two worlds, and men are caught in the middle with their dicks in their hands not knowing where to put them.

The real reason, I think, that my friends and all of society look down upon me and try to crush entrepreneurial women like myself is because I am a threat to their very system; the gravy train of handouts and the economy as a whole. Think about it for a second. What if men of this country suddenly felt it was O.K and "intelligent" to stop paying for dinners, drinks, houses, cars, shows and clothes for the Gold-Diggers and Green Bushes out there in hopes of getting some? That's right. Their lively hood, their whole existence, their life-blood would be cut-off because their value would go down. The pedestal would be lowered because with girls like myself there are no guessing and mind games; no ass-kissing self humiliation.

With me you know what you are getting. I will be what you want me to be, who you want me to be. I won't divorce and take half of your salary, your kids, your house, and your pension because I can't. What we are doing technically and legally doesn't exist.

There are no physical contracts between us, just the exchange of cash which has no trace; there are no receipts. I won't ever nag you, berate you, and cut you down in front of my friends and yours in public. I won't drag you to Bed Bath and Beyond on football Sunday; only after the game to my hotel room. I won't make you watch me try on sun-dresses at

Sears- only the one I will be taking off and tossing on the floor. I will never have a headache- besides the one you will give me from slamming the headboard. I will never ask you to take me out to places so I can show you off to my friends and make them jealous- only if you want me too. I will never give you ultimatums out of a biologically ticking fear- only if we have a safe word. I will never waste your time and your hard earned money on shiny trinkets- only if they are on the toys you want me to use.

I will never make you feel foolish babe because we are the two smartest, most honest people in one room, under one roof, in one American city.

I am societies dirty little secret.

FINAL FORECLOSURE

Los Angeles, California 2025

CALIFORNIA: FIND YOURSELF HERE is boldly plastered on a billboard outside on Mulholland in big enough lettering that can be seen from the window of my office opposite of the street. It wasn`t until tonight that I even noticed the sign, a sign that had been mocking me the entire time I have slaved away my life of countless precious hours in this godforsaken hellhole of gossip, backstabbing and legal covert prostitution.

People in this town don`t find themselves, if anything, the moment they land here with all their personal baggage is when they begin to die inside; lose themselves and who they once were in the sea of advertisements, business cards, meetings, and crocodile smiles. I am not sure what made me want to write this testament, confession, or ode to my nothing today. Maybe it's the half bottle of Pinot I found in the break-room, the fact that the entire city of L.A has been locked down from the coast to San Bernardino County, or because ever since the markets started bleeding points like a stuck pig my savings and clients have dried up quicker than the spot of wine I just spilled on my Vera Wang skirt.

Either way, here I am at age forty, divorced once, and living with my mom in a shitty condo on Mountain Drive off of West Kendall out in San Bernardino; a condo that is out of hopeless reach by now since the electricity has been cut, and the checkpoints are in firm places around the city. This is the first time I can say I've actually missed my mom. All those times I yelled at her to turn down her stupid soap operas, or for her trying to set me up with her friends grandsons seems like a distant memory now, and a waste of time that could have been better spent just bonding and getting to know her.

I never really knew her, my mom as a person; just as someone who ever step of the way in my life told me how I was doing everything wrong. From the men I've dated to even the outfit I picked out today to wear. She was right about most things though, I just didn`t want to admit it. Deep down she just wanted the best for me I guess, and now I can never tell her that. Tell her how I now understand it all, why our relationship has been like a bad sitcom episode.

I never really knew my dad. He passed away when I was only two. Mom said he died in the hospital from illness; however, I later found out secretly through my aunt Sara that he was a solvent abuser, cheated on my mom with hookers down in the Valley on those nights he said he`d be working late at the precinct. I never told my mom that I knew this, just like she never told me the truth; which is fine, she was just trying to protect me so that my life would never be haunted by the thought that my father, a man of the law, was a man of many sins.

My ex turned out to be a hopeless drunk who I have been still supporting to pay off our former house since both our names were on the mortgage. He doesn't have a cent to his name since that lawsuit at his work, and his now poisoned habit of drinking the pain away with cheap cases of Lone Star. I guess those payments don`t really matter now, which is an odd relief. He never hit or beat me, but it was as almost as if he did, since the emotional toll that our relationship took on me was like I had been beaten for years with soft punches on the inside.

Anyways, I don't know where he is now and what he is doing amidst all of the unrest in the streets; he is probably up at his brother's cabin near Mount Chiliad drinking and shooting his Colt at some poor wild-life or god knows what. I wouldn't be surprised if he is already dead wasting away in a ditch somewhere in the mountains with a trail of empties leading up to his body.

I guess it all doesn't really matter now. Did anything really matter? My life has been so hurried, so fast and busy that I had never taken the time to ask myself that question, yet here I am starring at that fucking billboard, alone, with this mediocre Pinot. What is there really to say? I'm sick of chauffeuring these fucking entitled wannabe playboys who have never worked a day in their life: Showing them properties that I could never purchase myself, and laughing at all their stupid jokes that I can't stand. All the while fending off their gropes; but not all their gropes because you never know, one of these days I might just get a full commission!

And you know what's hilarious? Well, people always joked about the lives of hookers and prostitutes because what they do is out in the open, advertised by years of common knowledge that when you drive up to that corner, or call that hotline, you know that sex is the commodity up for trade. Yet, what was I? What am I, a real-estate agent? No.

I was just as much a call-girl as those women I used to see on the corner while on house scouts. Everyone in this office was. Jessica, Kelly, Sasha, Marie and even Clay; It was like some sort of un-written code here that in order to make it big in this town you had to do some things you aren't proud of such as stealing clients from co-workers (even the new interns), all the way to blowing and fucking them at the locations to close the deal. All in the pursuit of what- a mansion near the yacht club and a fake social circle to go along with some fake breasts; the American Dream? Everyone steals and breaks the law I guess, it's what humans do. Some will admit it, and some will deny it. That`s why we invented locks and guns.

It's about 9:30 p.m. now, I am tired and I am afraid to go outside, not like I would make it far anyways. I feel like jumping. I don't know. I am tired, but not in the traditional sense of course. I am tired of having to eek my way through life, and especially in this world now. There is no reward for all the shit we do now in this country. The wanting to end it all now feels like how you would coming home after a long day- you just are so eager to hit the sheets. You want the world to go away, escape into the night, the slumber. It's different right now though, that feeling- one last midnight, that type of slumber.

A part of me thinks it would be hard, but my surroundings are telling me otherwise. Options are limited. I am sure to die, or worse taking by one of the mobs down there. I have no protection. I need a bad man, but a bad man who will protect me from the rest. The world needs bad men. It's twisted. I should have got out earlier. The cities are like rat traps when it all goes to shit. You're fucked.

All of those sporadic reports day after day of Wall Street types mysteriously winding up dead, committing suicide, and or just abruptly quitting and leaving their offices should have been a canary in the coal mine in hindsight. I think there is enough food in here to tie me over until at least the morning. The break room fridge still has some snacks and brown bags that people accidentally left or didn't eat from today. It's ironic that I am spending what is probably my last days in a place that has held me prisoner for so many years, yet it feels *ok*. It's no different now- the context just is. I should have left this country and city a long time ago- anywhere but here.

It's usually quite peaceful up here on a normal night- but there is a symphony of chaos down below. Every few minutes I can hear the sound of gun fire- cracks that rattle off the windows, muted and muffled by the thickness. Some I can tell are close by, others most likely across multiple blocks. The thuds and concussions of flash-bangs and grenades can be felt and heard thundering around the city like a distant lightning storm.

People are dying, I know it. Faint roars and yelling by the military can be heard and from the roaming gangs that have now formed. Women are screaming. Every now and then I can hear a real loud bang from high above our building- most likely a sniper with a high powered rifle. It could be military or someone else, that's the scary part. Nobody is in control of the situation. Nobody knows who is out there and what to do. The T.V's are down, radio, cell towers, internet, everything.

We are dark. Cut off. Nobody is telling us what to do anymore. People aren't being managed. This is what happens. Reality has collapsed. People panic without direction, stability, and hope- even if that hope was false in its fundamentals. Is this what 'freedom' really looks like? Can people ever be truly be free and do as they please, or are we incapable of self rule? What's worse, kissing the hand that feeds us, clothes us and manages us; a peaceful yet neo-feudal state, or a Darwinist battle-royal tribal factional free-for-all? Fuck it. God I am drunk. I have to get this down though. At least for me it's therapeutic. It's the loneliest feeling up here. The thought that nobody knows I am here and that I need saving. I feel so small, smaller than the dark shapes that litter the streets right now, just as dead. Just as insignificant.

I never actually took the time to appreciate how the hills looked in the foreground of the star filled sky, or how the moon casts a shimmer over the bay to make the water look as if a million fire-flies were dancing on its surface. It's now ruined with billowing smoke from torched out cars, and sporadic muzzle flashes from the darkened streets and alleyways that flash briefly and rapidly. It's actually quite sad in a way that it took the collapse of a nation to make me realize how beautiful this land really is, was. I wonder if anyone else is doing what I am doing at this hour, in this city or another, writing what will probably be never found or read by another human soul; their last days and moments, who they were as a person, and all their regrets. It's bullshit to me at least when people say they have no regrets in life. We all have regrets, and those who say they don't are only fooling themselves.

What are my regrets? Well for starters, marrying too young and to a drunk didn't help. I never got to see the Atlantic coast or travel overseas for that matter. I never truly felt loved or connected to anyone. The only thing I have ever felt connected to is this cesspool of a city, my Zoloft, the lying, and all the theatre that comes with it. Hell, I never even got to finish watching `Breaking Bad` to see how it all ended with Walter. That man, although a criminal, at least knew what he wanted, loved what he did, lived by his own rules, and was a genius at it. That's what I most regret I guess, not being me, whatever the fuck that is. I guess it's too late now to find out who the true Claire Rodgers is. For now, and forever, I am Claire, the alone, drunk, tired, and divorced real-estate agent in what is now the scariest place in America.

That billboard is really pissing me off right now because it's all starting to make sense. It mocks me like one of those information panels at the mall that show you your location, and how far you are away from the Gucci and Prada. `"California: Find yourself Here," well, I am here, and here is where I belong I guess. To whoever will find this...

Claire Rodgers – Sunny Palms Real Estate Inc

LOST TRANSMISSIONS

Sarasota County, Florida 2030

MESSAGE COULD NOT
BE DELIVERED TO RECIPIENT is forever pasted in
Marie's 'sent folder' to her husband who went
missing a year ago to this date. From her recollection,
everything was well between them, their lives
together and marriage. The messages sent prior to
Joseph's disappearance convinced Marie that all was
well with him, and that she would see him soon
shortly back at their once beautiful Floridian home
just outside of Sarasota.

```
"Just left the office Marie...picking up
those prints for your mother and I'll be
there soon" sent Jan 5 2026 at 5:11 pm
```

Joe had very little in the way of vices. He always
kept to himself while he was not in range of Marie's

embrace; he had no enemies that she could think of, and no signs of mental estrangement or illness. *Who would want to hurt Joe? Why would he leave me? Has he even left me?* She had been saying for quite some time now to herself. The detectives from the Sarasota County Sheriff's Office are bewildered as to what might have happened to Joe. No leads, no traces, and at this point there is little suspicion of foul play involved. They have even put "taps" on Joe's cell phone, credit cards and other means to which he would use to communicate and transmit to the outside world, to Marie, the police and anybody about his existence and whereabouts.

Since the disappearance, Marie has always felt slightly disconnected from the detectives involved in Joe's case, seeing as during one point in the investigation she felt as if she was being cross-examined given that no leads were turning up regarding her husband. The focus naturally became on her and their marriage. Soon after many attempts by the police, they left Marie and her family alone as they could not find any ounce of evidence, or motive towards Marie being involved in Joseph's now cold case file.

An astounding 4,300 Americans are reported missing every day, including both adults and children. But only a tiny fraction of those are stereotypical abductions or kidnappings by a stranger. It nags on Marie's mind; *People go missing all the time in America, how do we not know where they end up or go? The country is a virtual spy grid at the hands of the NSA, Google, Facebook and the Administration, so how is it that so many people are never found...they just disappear?*

When the Sheriff's Office found Joe's car it was almost as if he had not been in there. The vehicle seemed to have been wiped clean of all trace of human existence: finger prints, hair follicles, skin cells, ID, pocket change, used gum, and even Joe's stapled dream catcher that would always hang from the rear view mirror. Even more bizarre is that the Police told Marie that the car wouldn't even start. Everything, including the battery was dead. All the electronics seemed to have fried or short circuited by someone or something.

It's strange to think. One day someone's walking around, going to work, the grocery store, alive, and then nothing. People just disappear. It's as if the earth swallows them up whole, or they perhaps stumble upon a time portal or other dimension, never to be *found*, seen or heard from again.

Maybe they can still hear or see us, Marie likes to believe, and we for some reason can't seem to be able to do the same for them. They are still here with us, existing in anything and everything their soul and essence had come to touch on this place we call earth. People after all, our bodies flesh and thoughts, are just frequencies vibrating at different speeds to form its existence. We transmit these vibrations everyday when we are around others. How come it is that we feel a certain way around certain people? We know who the toxic people in our lives are because we can feel the darkness radiating off of them every time they are around us; their depression, anxiety, and hatred for themselves and their existence around others.

Then there are the people we feel an almost unearthly connection to, the ones who make us wonder if they are even human at all, and we secretly believe that perhaps they are angels sent down to make us and this world a whole lot better. Sometimes when we dream we can shape our waking realities, or complete other peoples sentences without even knowing what they are going to say next. It is all going on in the background, transmission of high and low signals, frequencies vibrating at unearthly speeds unable to be caught with the naked eye. They are like the signals of information that pass from satellites to our phones, T.V's, or computers. They travel so fast through the heavens; broken up into a million pieces and put back together again at a frequency that we can all see and hear.

Marie thinks of all this as she begins what has become an almost nightly ritual- driving to the place where she and Joe used to meet up when they were teenagers, lovers in a different time. It's just a short drive South, down the 301 past Ridge Wood Heights and Gulf Gate Estates located on the Siesta Key. They used to call it "The Tower" when they were young; an old WSLR 96.5 radio tower that still stands strong, and left upright since the city's coffers can't afford to tear it down since the greatest depression of 2025.

It's near the shoreline and on a clear night you can see for miles in every direction, the stars would wink and shimmer off the surf as the waves would calmly roll in amidst the warm night's breeze that would chill them in all the right places. Marie and Joseph used to come here sometimes with friends, but most nights it would be just the two of them, escaping a world of teenage angst, mild responsibilities and their overbearing and God-fearing parents. It was a spot and place they could declare their own. To share their thoughts, dreams and wonders of this life: Philosophy, tales of childhood shenanigans, and even sex would consume their time at the tower. It was a place to connect. A place they knew they could always find each other. A spot they could never be *found*.

Marie was always drawn to Joe. It was the way in which he was different from all the rest. He seemed worldly, but had not travelled outside of the state let alone the country. He seemed knowledgeable, yet never went to college or a University. He seemed to know her every wish, secret, wants and desires yet she was always conservative in her thoughts and feelings towards him when they first started to see each other. Joe just seemed to understand everything. He got it. Life. Everything. He was always calm and knew what to say without even thinking about it; this always made Marie uneasy at first about Joe but then couldn't help but continuously wonder why this was so with him. Marie will never forget though, as she looks up at the stars tonight at the old tower, what Joe said to her during one of their first times together:

"There will come a day when we will not be with each other, a time when we all must leave this place. I just want you to know that you will still have me with you always whatever shall become of this,"

She remembers him saying this one night they were talking about the stars and their existence to us. She thought that he meant when we die we will still be together in spirit or something of that nature, and she finds herself guessing if he actually meant the day that he would leave and disappear out of nowhere. Joe always loved talking about the stars and our connections to the extraterrestrial; Marie always loved to hear about it, she loved his voice.

Most of the stars we see above are ghosts, long dead before the light ever reaches earth and our eyes; we are essentially staring at history ever night, the death of something that once was there yet still lives on even after its demise. We stare at the past always. The moment we see something and by the time it takes the light and images to reach our eyes, it is already history. Everyday Marie looks into the mirror and sees her soft cheeks, her half-dried hair or the nail polish stains on her house robe, she is indeed starring at the past. She wishes Joe were there during those times to say this to her; as if speaking those words to her would somehow make that eerie fact comforting to her.

Now at the tower, she sits on top of the engineer hut and ponders this as she stares and scrolls through some of Joe's old texts. Her thoughts become scrambled now: *If we can't see something, does it not mean it isn't there? And just like the stars, if we can still see something, does it still remain so, alive?* The black texts from Joe's words on her phone are accentuated by the darkness of tonight and the alien glow that her phone emits. It haunts her every time she stares at those words; a part of him is still alive in that phone.

She calls him all the time just to hear his voice mail, and still sends him texts in the vein hope that they will go through, to wherever he is. She thinks of all the electronic signals and messages that are trapped in all of the other lost phones, waiting to be opened. They are trapped in some database or satellite in the sky, waiting to be sent and only to be terminated once the phone company cuts service to that lost inactive number. The day that happens to Joe's number will be the hardest for Marie because that will be the last tangible connection severed.

There is a place Marie likes to hide that's in all of our minds. It's in the dark of the night when everyone is a sleep. It's well known that we all can have a brittle heart, and cracks in our spirit. It's deep inside all of us and it has a sound that we can follow in hopes of attaining clarity. It feels like we've hit a barrier, but we will survive. And it will always be hard for us to swallow. We have all been to that place before. A place where we can feel either the most comfort or an extreme anxiety; where nobody can hear us, see us, annoy us, envy us, want us, use us or need us to be something that is not our own destiny. We still live on.

We have all been lost before, not wanting to be *found*.

A MILLENNIAL
IN DRIFT

Chicago O'Hare International Airport 2008

Tidal Wave (feat. Alpines) begins to fill my headphones with its sawed ambient synthesizers and carefree lyrics as I wait for my direct to Frankfurt Germany. My boss wasn't too impressed when I gave him barely five days notice that I wouldn't be continuing my life fulfilling job as a hostess at Montana's, along with my suburban lifestyle.

I guess that's what happens when you have epiphanies about the state of your affairs and life in general. Everything comes at you so quickly. The realizations that I had after graduation washed over me so fast that I just couldn't wait to consult Trip

Advisor and start making my reservations for a new adventure, a new life.

The awareness of moving back home with my parents scares me to death, along with the realization that my degree in International Studies (with a Minor in Women's Studies) is pretty much worthless; a very expensive piece of paper with fancy raised lettering, font and title. Actually, that's a bit of a white lie. The main reason why I want to escape is because of my boyfriend, my ex-boyfriend to be exact.

Everything started off in the typical way most millennial relationships do- We met back in first year at this 'Tight and Bright' 80's party my friend "Cat" (short for Kate) threw during 'reading week'. We were both drunk and high on life, among other things. It was the way he gazed into my eyes while we danced like fools to Eric Carmen's "Make Me Lose Control," and the way he thought my lip synching to Pat Benatar's "Shadows of the Night" was sexy; along with how my neon leggings flattered my every curve (thanks school gym membership!).

Like your typical hormonal and self-gratifying Twenty-Something's we hooked up that night, and stayed together for the 4 remaining years.

I wasn't normally the one to be in a relationship- I have always been a free-spirit in a way. However, stupidly I felt the need to force a relationship with this guy because all my roommates and friends had boyfriends, and I felt like the odd one out, like there was something wrong with me.

Things started off great with him; his name was Mike. I guess I can say his name now since not mentioning it isn't going to erase the past or give me a much needed onset of Alzheimer's. Anyways, like I said, things were great in the beginning. Everything from dates to the sex was filled with passion and mystery. He was a mystery. Then the honeymoon phase started to fade fast like daylight during the winter months, and things got stale. We started to become a typical couple doing typical couple things; like going on double dates, gossiping about other couples, and binge watching Netflix Originals. He didn't seem to mind, but I did. I thought I could be that person, that kind of woman.

However, deep down I knew I would be miserable if I continued this charade, this programmed post-

Industrial Revolution way of life that had existed for sole purpose of rebuilding a nation after a world war. The world doesn't need saving anymore. I don't need saving as a woman. We live in a time where the survival of humans doesn't depend on everybody procreating.

I had a huge falling out with my friend Kate, along with my other roommates who all belong to that camp of "happily ever after," and "I've found *my* boo, where's yours?" cult. I don't need a "boo," and I depend on having one. I actually find living independently an easier life-style choice then having to live or be with someone for the long haul. I don't have to worry about pleasing someone's every wish and emotion. I don't have to take care or be responsible for someone else's mess or trauma. Am I being selfish you ask? Well, to be honest, I think it is selfish for people to depend on someone else for their own happiness. To rely on someone for something that can be generated by the self is foolish to me, and is a recipe for depression in my eyes. Surly it is nice to have someone to share things with, but I wouldn't have someone around because I couldn't function without them. What do I know though? I am just a dumb 22 year old girl right? With age comes wisdom you say? That's bullshit. With age comes dementia and bitterness, and I already have one of those qualities; so I think I am well qualified to give my thoughts.

My roommates on the other hand seem like they can't or don't know how to function on their own. I don't even think that any of them have been alone or on their own for more than 3 months in their lives. My roommate Amber for instance has a new boyfriend within a week of the last, and Kirsten also falls into the category of having to be constantly on the prowl for new "D" every time a guy dumps her. What really pissed me off, and what was the real reason for our falling out, was the way in which they felt it was their duty to give me relationship/boy advice. For being "progressive" women as they all claimed, their thinking and actions resembled something of a backwards nature, something that tossed 40 years of progress for women out the window.

Amber always used to talk about her "90 day rule" with guys in order to make sure that they would stay around and commit to the relationship. She was clearly delusional. She thought that if you made a guy wait for sex and first made him "invest" in the relationship (dates, gifts, time, dinners, and money) then he will be more likely to stick around for the long haul since he has already invested so much. Well, I remember having a big fight with her over this, and telling her that it doesn't matter how long it takes for sex to happen. A guy could just as easily leave you after 6 months as in one day. Also, I told her that the way in which she went about relationships was extremely manipulative, cold and calculating.

To coerce a man into a relationship by getting him to invest enough "time, money and effort" before sleeping with him seems incredibly conniving and cold. Surely the man should embark on a relationship with you because he likes *you* not because he'll feel like he's wasted time, money, and effort if he doesn't? The wasted time, money, and effort principle is actually very prevalent in both gambling -slot machine/fruit machines- and in financial scams where they are utilized to extract as much cash from individuals as possible, hardly a good principle to use in your search for a meaningful relationship. I also told her that she single handily was sending women back into the past be promoting these actions; treating men and herself like a John and a hooker. Basically I told her that the 90 day rule is equivalent to that of legal prostitution. You should have seen her face, it was priceless.

Sure enough, Amber wanted nothing to do with me after saying such a thing, and wouldn't even talk to me for the rest of the semester; I guess the truth hurts when someone calls a spade a spade. We don't need to act like this anymore as women. If we want a relationship with someone, we better let that person know from the very beginning, if we just want to have fun and have sex we should also convey this too (a mistake I made) so that both parties don't end up miserable for lying to themselves about what they really want. The other thing I couldn't understand about Amber was how she could wait 90 frigging days without "getting some." What woman would put herself through that sort of unnecessary torture? Women like sex and need it just as much as guys; its O.K to admit this, it isn't 1800's anymore ladies.

Anyways, I don't know how this song Tidal Wave made it on to my itunes in the first place; someone must have added it to my player at one of the parties I threw (You know like when people get too drunk and want to blast their favorite playlist/song for everyone to hear). I like it though. It's starting to grow on me. The music in a way is illustrating what I am going through, my life and what I want to be right now: The bass-synth, and the way it is sluggish and lurching, reminds me of everyone I am leaving behind, their lives and how they are a constant struggle into boringness. I want to become like that leading synth sound; it enters in so smooth, so boldly and catches your ear in just the right way as it cries out for the strength to overcome everything. It's the sound of freedom breaking through the chains of society, the thing we all want.

If things stay the way they are, life is over at this point. Not literally. What I mean is, everyone I know will go through college with their worthless incubated degrees. Or, get knocked up at some dorm-room kegger only to then migrate back to their home town a few years from now and move into one of these cookie-cutter houses- Only to then pump out little versions of themselves to which perpetuates the mediocre cycle of suburban servitude.

That's something I think people all tend to forget when they get caught up in the rat-race and expectations of their bosses, in-laws, partners and parents. I think they forget (as I have) that life is to be lived on your own terms, and not on someone else's. This world is ours for the taking. We were born and put on this earth to explore its pleasures and bounties. The earth is a platter of the finest of pleasures that need to be tasted; a veritable banquette of flavorful notes and existence.

People need to get rid of the word "should." That word has messed up so many people's lives and futures. It's a word that will make you depressed and end up like the 1 in 4 women who take anti-depressants in America. I hear it all the time from my grandparents, parents, and even some of my close friends. "Melissa, you're so beautiful and attractive how come your not married by now?" or my favorite "When I was your age I had a full-time job and was married, what's wrong with you?" Well, I can tell you what's wrong with *you*, you're fucking delusional comparing my generation to yours and your parents before you.

After all, it's *your* generation that has caused this mess we are in, and you have the elitist audacity to ask me what my problem is? It was *your* bankers, *your* politicians and *you're* thinking that has raped *our* future. Thanks for the 50% unemployment rate among 18-30 year olds, the allowing of a globalist take-over of the world, and the out-sourcing of culture and jobs. If anything my problem is *you*. Live your life and I will live mine, instead of trying to suck me into your miserable greedy void so you can feel better about your life choices in being "the right path." News Flash: There are no right paths in life, this is all one giant lucid dream, and we are the architects of our own stories. We wake up when we die, so we should enjoy it while it lasts.

They are calling my gate number now finally. It's about time too since I've had a bit too many at the bar here in A terminal. I really hope Europe is as loose and carefree as people say. I have heard the pace of everything over there is much different than ours. People don't rush around everywhere like they do in Chicago; they take their time to enjoy the idle moments of life. I hope I meet people who aren't so tightly wound and conniving as they are here in America. I figure I will make money on the go as I travel, doing anything (waiting tables, washing dishes, working vineyards), I don't really care. I want to work to live and not the other way around. A job to me is an afterthought, like washing your hands before a good meal.

I want to meet different men, experience different people and explore my wants and desires. I don't want to be part of the human farm we call modern society. I am tired of all the cookie-cutters, the bro's and the typical. Give me different, give me surprises, and give me life. Don't give me average, routine, what's "expected," and what "Should be." I don't want my life's story to be some third-string garbage you would read in the "Life" section of the Tribune. I want it to be a page turner.

I need it to be *my* master piece.

Made in the USA
Charleston, SC
02 February 2016